Of Cypress &
Sunflowers

Of Cypress & Sunflowers

Henry Henkel

Other Islands Press

OTHER ISLANDS PRESS

128 South Mill Road, Princeton Junction, NJ 08550

Library of Congress catalog data available upon request.
Library of Congress Control Number: 2015943121

Printed in the United States of America

EAN: 978-0-9749733-3-3
First Printing
ISBN: 0-9749733-3-5

For Patrick Eagan, the truest man I have ever met.

Contents

Lt. Col. Barney Shelby, Retired • 1

The End • 31

Cellulite Becomes Her • 41

Easter Sunday in the Suburbs • 91

Hannah Sue • 105

Of Cypress & Sunflowers • 141

The King • 175

Life Comes to Spring • 199

The Waters of San Sebastiano • 239

Timothy Harper • 273

Lt. Col. Barney Shelby, Retired

B arney's bald head was tilted against the side of the barn. He sat atop a bale of hay while droplets of sweat formed slow-moving rivulets that eventually converged and dripped off of his chin. Four small dogs were arranged randomly on the ground to his left. One of the dogs was attached to another with a frayed bit of green twine. The remaining two dogs walked in random orbits around each other. From a distance, they looked like a small cluster of satellites circling the orb that was Barney.

Barney wore a brown flannel shirt with sleeves rolled up to the elbow. Sweat soaked through every available piece of cloth. There was a faded white cooler parked on Barney's right that also seemed to be sweating. Droplets of condensation lined the top of the poorly sealed cooler.

Eyes closed, Barney appeared to be sleeping. In fact, he was thinking and listening. He heard nothing. The air was thick with heat and humidity, but not a sound could be heard. Barney's eyes popped open wide.

"Goddamn!" He screamed so loudly that the satellite dogs recoiled in fear. "Goddamn! What happened to the Goddamn crickets?"

Even the dogs seemed to survey their limited horizon in a state of confusion. Perhaps they were just surprised by the sudden increase in the noise level.

"The damn crickets!" Barney looked at the dogs for affirmation or confirmation, and then spat at one of them in disgust.

"How is it that a day can be as hot as this 'un and the damn crickets have decided to stop their damn chirpin'? Maybe they had a group heart attack or sumthin'. The damn vermin were chirpin' up a storm no more than ten minutes ago…now? Nuthin'! What in the name of Jesus H Christ is goin' on? It is hotter than hell, goddamn it." Barney looked at the dogs again. The dogs all eyed each other silently and offered Barney no intelligent response.

Barney stood up and ran his hand over his sweaty head and wiped his sweat-soaked hand on his pants. He looked at the barn, the haystack, and the cooler, and shook his head in disgust. A catbird began to call from the peak of his barn roof. Barney searched for a stone on the ground and launched it at the bird. The bird flew away and silence returned to the barnyard.

Barney stared at the forest that bordered his farm. He believed that all crickets lived in the forest.

He squinted to see if he could spot them. The dogs formed a straight line beside their master and looked toward the forest just as he did. Barney spat over the head of one of them and the line was quickly broken.

"Oh, the hell with it. I need me a beer." Being alone on the farm for so long, Barney didn't realize he was speaking out loud to himself any more. He was a modern day Ben Gunn, in retreat, not in exile. He reached into the cooler and pulled out a bottle. He looked at the label and sighed. "Look at this beer… can't drink the Frenchman's beer. Hate the damn Frenchman's beer. Need a bottle opener to get at the Frenchman's beer. Damn Frenchman's beer…."

Barney reached in for a different bottle of beer. "Goddamn that Frenchman! Drank all my beer he did, left this crap behind." He searched through the ice water and finally found a beer he could call his own.

A smile crossed his face as he twisted the cap off the top of his beer and began to drink. Holding the cap between his thumb and middle finger, he launched it at the dogs and hit one of them between his fore and hind legs. Barney chuckled and drank some more beer. He was now feeling less hot. The silent crickets had been forgotten.

After a time, Barney reached into the cooler and found nothing left but "the Frenchman's beer." Resolved to choking down as much as he could, he looked for the bottle opener in its usual spot attached to the handle of his other cooler. He went inside his cabin to fetch it.

"Goddamn it!" Barney's scream echoed in his small cabin. The dogs, roused from their mid-afternoon siesta, formed a tight circle of fear beside the white cooler. "The Frenchman drinks my damn beer and steals my damn bottle opener. Harpo, Hoppy, Helen, Whoever, c'mon! We are going to go see the Frenchman about a beer."

Having been roused by all the racket served by Barney, it wasn't hard for the dogs to fall into line behind their master. Barney grabbed a beer from the cooler as evidence. Together, the five walked the dry, dusty road that led to the Frenchman's barn.

• • •

The Frenchman sat outside his barn speaking to a visitor who had arrived recently from the coast. While they were speaking, the Frenchman spied Barney and the dogs approaching. He held his hand up to pause his visitor's speech.

"My neighbor and his dogs approach. Something is up. They never walk this far, especially on such a hot day."

The visitor turned and saw the odd troop approaching. Being a cautious man, he asked his friend if he should go inside the house. The Frenchman said nothing, shook his head slightly, and with a slight movement of his left hand directed his friend to stand by his side. As the group got closer, the visitor was surprised to see that two of the dogs held leashes for the other two dogs—it was as if they were walking the others. Upon closer examination, the visitor noticed that one of the dogs had only three legs!

The Frenchman hissed as the group drew nigh, "Remain silent and enjoy the show."

Barney did not stop walking until he was about two paces before the Frenchman. He had not yet said a thing. Crickets were chirping in a dense clump of ferns that the Frenchman had planted near the corner of his barn. A slight breeze blew the thinning hair of the visitor from the coast. The dogs stood in a single line behind Barney as he read the words that had been painted on the side of the Frenchman's barn. Two short paragraphs, painted in black, had caught Barney's attention. Before addressing the Frenchman and his visitor, Barney read them aloud.

"Please continue to smoke your cigarettes and chew your tobacco. Smoke and chew every day. Join my nephew who died too young from smoking and chaw. He loved his tobacco, too.

"Please continue to take your drugs. Shoot your heroine. Enjoy the life that drugs will give you. Join my niece who died too young from a drug overdose. She loved her drugs, too."

When he had finished reading, Barney summoned up some spit from the chaw that was in his mouth and spit at the dogs, hitting the three-legged dog right between the eyes. The dog whimpered and tried to wipe the spit off his face with both paws. He fell to the ground and dragged the dog to which he was attached with him.

Barney eyed the Frenchman and his friend with disdain. "You are one sanctimonious piece of garbage, Frenchman! What the hell is all this stuff about?"

The Frenchman looked at Barney. "I did it for my brother-in-law, their father, him." The Frenchman pointed to the man that Barney did not know. "His children are dead from drugs and tobacco."

Barney's gaze was diverted to the face of the visitor that had grown gaunt and hardened by this uncomfortable moment. The visitor did not look at Barney. He looked at the ground before him.

Not being one to retreat from a position, Barney spoke briefly but with confidence. "Yah. Hah. I am sure they are in a better place." The visitor nodded silently without moving his gaze from the ground.

Barney returned his gaze to the Frenchman. He pulled an unopened bottle of beer from his pocket. "Know what this is? This is your crap beer. You brought it to my cooler. Remember?"

The Frenchman nodded. "Last week."

"Yeah…last week. You drank my damn beer. You left me with this crap. This is all I have left now. Know what else? You took my damn bottle opener! Even if I wanted to drink this crap, I can't because you stole my bottle opener, you French sonofabitch." Spittle flew from his mouth as he spoke and sweat was flung everywhere as he gesticulated to make his point.

The Frenchman smiled wryly. "Not a social call then? Didn't want to stop by for some friendly chatter?"

Barney glared at the Frenchman and shot a menacing look at his friend before he responded. "A social call? No, this ain't no goddamn social call. I want my damn bottle opener."

Barney spat at a different dog and hit him squarely on the snout. The dog collapsed immediately and wiped his snout feverishly, trying to remove the foreign juice from his face before it dried. Without thinking, Barney grabbed the chaw of over-chewed tobacco from between his teeth and gums and tossed it in the general direction of the Frenchman's ferns. Suddenly, the crickets stopped chirping. Barney reached into his pocket and inserted some fresh chew. He squinted at the Frenchman and his friend and spat, just missing the one dog who had not yet been stained with his tobacco juice.

The Frenchman's friend thought it time to change the subject to ease the tension of the moment. "Those are mighty nice dogs you got there, well-trained too. Coming through the field, it looked like they were paired up, walking each other." He tried to smile at the implacable Barney. "What are their names?"

Barney squinted at the stranger before he began his answer. "Nice dogs...yeah, nice dogs." His voice was dripping with sarcasm. "Where are you from anyway?"

"What?" The stranger was confused.

"You know...." Barney's eyes grew wide for emphasis. "Where do you live? House...apartment? I'm guessing California."

The air that was taken in by the Frenchman became an audible hiss. Barney glared at him.

"Stay out of this, frog boy. I'm talkin' to your friend here."

The friend seemed a bit unsettled. He had wandered into an invisible minefield of awkward conversation. He had no idea how an expression like "nice dogs" could be construed so negatively by the stranger before him. The stranger's stare was so intimidating that he felt oddly defensive about the city in which he lived.

Finally, the Frenchman's friend answered, " I am from San Francisco. I wonder how that connects to your nice dogs, though."

"You wouldn't know..." Barney spat in disgust and hit the dog who had just finished cleaning his snout right back on the snout again. The dog wiped its nose furiously and rolled on its back in frustration.

"What does that mean?" The Frenchman's friend was feeling put upon by this man he had just met.

Barney chuckled a bit and spit right between the feet of the Frenchman's friend who jumped back instinctively.

Barney laughed again. He held the gaze of the Frenchman's friend a second more than one normally would. Barney knew why, Barney chuckled again and began to speak. "Well, that one, she's Helen, named her for Helen Keller. That dog is blind as a bat." He spat in Helen's general direction but she did not move, because she did not see the spit flying.

"Hoppy, that's the three-legged cur. He can see real good, so I taught him to lead Helen around. As you can see, he is one leg short of a table so I thought that Hoppy was a real good name for him."

"Over there, the one with the spots, that's Harpo. I have never heard that dog bark once in all the years I have had him. Never barks a syllable — damndest thing. I taught Harpo to help Whoever —that's the dog with the full brown snout." Barney spat on the dog's nose for emphasis, causing the dog to yelp a bit as it endeavored to clean itself off. Barney chuckled at the dog struggling to remove the tobacco juice.

"Interesting names… Why do you call that one Whoever?

For a moment Barney forgot himself and he gave the Frenchman's friend straight answer. "Oh…Well Whoever over there is deaf as a post. That's why Harpo leads him around. I figured Whoever was a good name because it don't really matter what you call a dog that can't hear a damn thing you're saying."

The stranger smiled at Barney and looked at the odd collection of dogs before him.

Barney's attention returned to the Frenchman. "Went to town yesterday. Saw that Stevens finally opened up his 'Dollar Store'."

"Really?" The Frenchman was just beginning to reengage. His mind had been diverted by the relaxing sound of the crickets chirping in his ferns.

"Yeah, that dumb sonofabitch. He has a big neon sign that says 'DOLLAR STORE' in big green letters right across the whole front of the damn store. Then, right below that sign, he has a big printed sign that says, 'Everything is $1.19'…How stupid can one man be?"

The Frenchman shook his head in absent-minded agreement but his friend from California decided it was time to be funny. "Maybe one dollar is just the manufacturer's suggested retail price."

Barney's eyes formed a very tight squint as they focused on the stranger before him. "Did you just say sumthin'?"

The stranger repeated his joke, emphasizing to Barney that it was… "just a joke."

The Frenchman shook his head and stared at the ground on his right.

Barney's icy glare yielded a cold, hard question for the Frenchman's friend. "Hobos or Homeless???"

"What?" The man from San Francisco had no idea how this conversation had just turned to this inane place.

"Hobos or Homeless, what are they?"

The stranger from California decided to engage. "Everybody knows that those who need homes are homeless. 'Hobo' is just an anachronistic term. The hobo is an icon of a lost era."

The Frenchman shuffled uneasily and thought it might be time to leave, but he couldn't abandon his friend. As he sat there, waiting for what he was certain would be another "Barney blow up," his mind turned to Hiroshima. If they knew the bomb was coming, no one would have stayed, would they? Didn't we drop leaflets and tell them to leave, tell them that death was coming from on high? But they stayed, didn't they? They didn't stay to help their friends. They stayed because they couldn't believe what was going to take place would take place. The truth unexperienced could not possibly be true. We know what to say and think about the past because we have already experienced it. We have no method of understanding the future. The future has no context. Barney, on the other hand, was always in context, always predictable. What his friend was about to experience, the Frenchman knew too well. It was never pretty, but he knew that he had to stay as a show of support for the visitor from the coast.

"An icon of a lost era? An anachronism…? Is that right?" Barney was seething. He spat tobacco juice twice in rapid succession, soiling both Harpo and Whoever. They didn't have a chance to move. This time they ran away to create some distance between themselves and Barney so that they could clean up in peace.

"Perhaps my little friend from San Francisco needs to be educated about what a Hobo is…"

The stranger interrupted Barney, "I think I know what a hobo is."

Barney glared at the man one more time and said, "I don't think you do." Barney spat on a cricket that he couldn't see. The Frenchman sighed silently and tilted his head against the side of his recently painted barn.

"A hobo, my friend from the city, is much more than an icon of a lost era. A hobo is America. America when she was powerful. America when she was happy. America when her enthusiasm for hard work and growth knew no bounds."

The stranger smirked and interrupted Barney again. "You realize that a hobo is no more than a vagrant, a glorified bum."

"Book wise and stupid all wrapped up into one. Maybe you should open yourself up a '$1.19 with suggested retail $1.00 store.'" Barney let his head shake sarcastically as he spoke to the stranger. "What you don't seem to understand is that the hobo understood the glory of America. This 'bum' knew he could ride the 3:10 freight train to anywhere and find work, find friends, find company, find America in places where you wouldn't even know where to look! The power of America enabled the hobo to have the confidence to strike out to find something different, something meaningful because there was so much 'there' there. It wasn't only the people either, people willing to share, to help, to contribute to the rhythm of the rails that the hobo rode upon. It was the majesty of nature's cathedral; the hobo saw it, the hobo lived it, the hobo sought it out. The hobo found the answers of the marketplace, which are generally not nearly as meaningful as the silent absorption of their spirit in Nature. 'This land is your land, this land is my land' – ever hear it???"

"Yes, yes of course." The stranger was shocked and a little bit intimidated by Barney's love of the hobo.

"Did it mean nothing to you? Was it just words on a page? Mindless meanderings of some trivial artistic spirit? Could you not feel the love? Could you not feel the expansive nature of the country in the lyrics of the song? One can't imagine freedom, love and enthusiasm, he must experience it. With limited possessions and a lot of heart these spirits took to the road, not worried about dying because of America's ability to care for its own. The hobo only worried about not living enough."

"They were covered with the dirt of Thomas Jefferson, Thomas Paine, Nathan Hale. They smelled the smoke of the creation of industry, the growth of

America. They smelled the clear air of the Tetons and the Rockies while burning Pino wood in some freight car to keep warm."

"What of the homeless? Do they not experience all or some of these same things today?"

Barney spat so violently that it knocked Hoppy right off his feet when it struck him. The stranger could barely see his eyeballs as Barney unveiled his tightest squint yet. "You said it yourself. The 'homeless' are without a home. The homeless populate every city, every town in America, but they don't live here. What song about America have you heard from a 'homeless' man recently? They station themselves by bureaucratic buildings built in the Sixties—faceless, vacant, and dependent—waiting for a check that will allow them to survive until the next one comes along. They live a life of one damn thing after the other, doing nothing, experiencing drugs and dependency. Dependency on the government worker with bad shoes walking out of one these Auschwitz gray buildings to give them the handout that justifies their life as a victim. A hollow, vacant, emotionally scarred vessel that is empty. The homeless are sustained by guilt— the guilt of those who have more. Guilt and Pity are emotions most vile. They are feelings only experienced by those who are superior to those for whom they feel the emotion. Today's 'homeless' man is emblematic of what America has become, a large empty vessel, vapid in its dependency on emotion and material goods, papering over our faults, making excuses for our lack of drive, sense of purpose, and true feeling of community." Barney spat again and hit nothing. The stranger thought that a wistful look seemed to cross his face as Barney stared out over the fields surrounding the Frenchman's house.

"Maybe you are right. Maybe you are right." Barney scrubbed some of the sweat off of his chin as he thought. "Maybe the role of the homeless man in America today is the same as it was when the hobo roamed the country. Maybe that's true. What a pity. America may be the one that changed. Maybe she changed right before my eyes and I never noticed. Never took the time to see, to evaluate, to realize that she was changing right in front of me and she wasn't particularly interested in me or anything that I thought or valued anymore." Barney scrubbed his chin and looked at the ground again. "How did I miss that? It's a pretty goddamn big thing to miss, isn't it?" He shook his head in disgust.

The stranger thought that Barney may have teared up at the end of his speech. He had no idea whether they were still talking about Hobos or the homeless or America anymore. He was thinking that the conversation may have just taken another left turn and that he had now wandered into that torture chamber which is Barney's brain. He was grateful that the Frenchman took that moment to rejoin the conversation.

"You didn't really come over here to talk about the hobos now, did you, Barney? You came over here for some other purpose, isn't that right?" The Frenchman knew Barney well enough and cared about him. He didn't want Barney to realize that he had allowed the Frenchman's friend from San Francisco to see him this way.

"That's right, you thievin' sonofabitch!" Barney had regained his focus. "Where in the hell is my damn bottle opener? While you are at it, you'd think you'd offer me a damn beer. It's hot out. In case you haven't noticed, the crickets are chirpin' up a freakin' storm. Now toss me damn beer and a good one too. Not one of your damn foo foo beers."

The Frenchman obliged Barney and passed another beer to his friend also. The friend had returned to his 'safe spot' in the discussion, which was right beside the Frenchman. His mind had been tossed so many different ways that he couldn't wait to speak to the Frenchman about all they had discussed and experienced with this strange man today.

Within what seemed to be seconds to the stranger from the coast, Barney had finished his beer. He tossed the empty bottle to the Frenchman who caught it with his left hand while drinking with his right. The stranger had barely sipped his beer, but the Frenchman was halfway done when Barney asked for another. He twisted off the cap, squeezed it between his two fingers and shot it at Hoppy. It flew right by where his fourth leg would have been. Barney wiped the corner of his mouth and muttered, "Woulda hit a damn dog with a full set of wheels." He spit in Hoppy's general direction.

Hoppy shambled away slowly looking emotionally hurt by the words of his master.

Barney drank half a beer and stared over the field from which he and the dogs had just come. Without looking at the Frenchman, he began to speak. "Was thinking about Velvet Melvin the other day. Remember that crazy sonofabitch?"

The Frenchman nodded absentmindedly, and drank more of his beer. "Velvet Melvin…sure. Vodka, tequila, and beer. The Sandwich Ich and Mardi Gras Purple. Who could ever forget Velvet Melvin." He drank some more beer and smiled. This was the shorthand conversation of two old friends. Full sentences and complete thoughts were a waste of time. Time was something they didn't have much of. The sense of Velvet Melvin was sufficient to have them both nodding together about times long gone and memories shared. Both men smiled to no one.

The stranger had finished almost one-eighth of his beer and realized he was in a fog again. The conversational experiences he had had so far made him fearful to ask, but he had to know. "For the love of Mike, what are you two talking about now?" He took a full gulp of beer for emphasis.

"Love of Mike, that's San Francisco speaking." Barney responded with a devilish grin that creased his face as the Frenchman rolled his eyes and the dogs looked at Barney quizzically. "Well, for the love of Mike then…"

By now the visitor had "gotten" Barney's homophobic humor. It was his turn to squint at Barney. "It's an Irish saying, you Neanderthal sonofabitch."

Barney laughed out loud and looked at the Frenchman while he spoke, "OK…OK…Jeez, give a little man a little beer and he gets all sensitive on us." He winked at the Frenchman and began the tale of Velvet Melvin.

"Velvet Melvin served with us overseas. He was a big black dude who could crush almost anything with his bare hands. When we got back home, nothing was real enough for Melvin. He was always looking to do something different than everyone else. He opened up a bar called 'Velvet Melvin's Specialty House' which served Tequila, Vodka and beer —nothin' else. No mixers, no soda, nuthin' —— only those 3. He'd have country bands come in to play and it was like the fuckin' Wild West. Beer bottles flyin', tequila being guzzled by the bottle — it was wild. The whole inside of the place was painted black and the only light came from candles on tables that people used to heave at the band and at each other —it was great. Then, he opened up a sandwich place called The Sandwich Ich, but – no one wanted to eat there cause they couldn't understand what the name meant and they were scared. Melvin understood people better than anyone." Barney laughed again.

The Frenchman who was now on his second beer silently nodded in agreement. Barney wasn't tellin' the story very well but he could fill in the blanks with his own memories of the places and the people.

The stranger didn't get it. So he tried a different tack. "What about the 'Mardi Gras Purple?'"

Without Barney asking, the Frenchman tossed a beer into Barney's left hand. Barney continued to speak. "Melvin is the only sonofabitch I know north of N'awlins who decorated his damn house for the Mardi Gras. Most common assholes put out decorations for Christmas and Halloween —Melvin ONLY decorated for Mardi Gras. He'd put masks around his front door, purple and green lights on his bushes. Masks on windows and in trees; it was amazing. One year he decided it wasn't enough. He painted the entire inside of his house Mardi Gras purple — deep purple. Every goddamn thing—purple. My God, it was beautiful." Barney shook his head as he looked backed over the field.

For the first time, it was the Frenchman's turn to laugh. "Yeah…It was goddamn beautiful." Both men laughed together and the visitor from the coast had no idea about what was so funny. Barney looked at the stranger with renewed intensity and scrubbed his chin while he stared. "Guess you had to be there… guess you had to be there."

Barney had perceived the confusion of this visitor he had just met. The heat and the alcohol were creating a calming mix in his system and he tried to engage the stranger one more time.

"You've got to embrace it all, my cowardly little friend. You have to make yourself feel that you are a part of something special. If we are only average, why live? If we all avoid the unknown, the scary, why live? If we only spend our life burnishing the mediocre, hiding from the challenging, then why live? If your schematic for life is to forget the thirties, have kids in the forties, be sick between the fifties and sixties, and figure out where to die after that, then why live? The Frenchman is a lazy good for nuthin' asshole, but at least he tried…he tried to be sumthin' Why do you think an artist tries to paint?"

The visitor had no idea where this conversation was going and found himself afraid to answer Barney's question. "I'm not sure why. Never really thought about it, I guess…."

Barney was exasperated all over again. "Never really THOUGHT about it??? Really…?" Hey Frenchman, why is this mutherfucker here?"

Silently, the Frenchman shrugged his shoulders.

"The point of painting, my friend, is to capture the moment that never exists again, even though it may take weeks to capture it perfectly. So how the hell do you capture 'a moment' when it takes so long to do it? Brady made people sit for hours. Monet could not do that. You heard of him right? The guy was a painter."

The stranger rolled his eyes and nodded his head simultaneously.

Barney continued, "There were endless seconds worthy of memory flashing before his eyes and he had to capture them as quickly and accurately as he could because he knew that they were already gone and soon he would be gone, and then the memories would be gone. The beauty, the travesty, the moment, the light, the darkness, the life, the pain, the joy, the sorrow, all gone -—all captured. All gone and forgotten unless you paint the picture. Unless you remember the moment and retell it. It is all lost unless you experience it, then share it, then hope there is some particle of understanding of what you are trying to convey, what you are trying to do... We sit beside Monet and see what he sees for that moment. But that is not enough...We have to see it ourselves. Know it, live it, be it. I know all because I have lived all that I have experienced. I lived it! He had cataracts, you know..."

The stranger could barely keep up with Barney's inebriated tirade. "Who had cataracts?"

"Monet, you dolt. At the end... Look at the pictures of early morning and fog and ice floes. You can see it if you let yourself experience it. Why was he out at 3 AM with a hot stove and a paintbrush. Do you have any idea? Why would he paint the fog??? Why spend so much time capturing that which is less than dramatic?"

The stranger had only come to visit the Frenchman. He wasn't prepared for all this. Only flip answers crossed his brain, but he thought that if he gave a flip answer, Barney might kill him. Acquiescent silence, limited oral interaction and withdrawal seemed to be the best strategy. Striving to adopt this minimalist attitude, he simply said, "Why?"

Barney was beside himself with frustration. For some unknown reason, the dogs had roused themselves and stood in a straight line beside him. "Because he knew what was beautiful. Because he knew that he was going to die." As he spoke this sentence, it seemed that all the bluster and intensity that was Barney had been exhausted. He looked weary and dejected. Still, he continued to speak, "He knew he was going to die. He knew it was going to be over. All he had seen, all he had been, disappearing from the landscape. Who would know now if he didn't paint the picture of where he had been and what he had seen. It wasn't really important that those who appreciated his work would know. It was much more important that he would know. He was part of the landscape because he was able to paint it. We can remember Velvet Melvin because we stood beside him, fought the same battles, experienced what we thought were the same victories, laughed at the same funny situations."

The Frenchman raised his bottle to toast Barney, "Right on, brother."

The colloquialism struck the stranger as being quaint, funny, and poignant all at once. His view of the language and the world was so much different than these two men. He appreciated it, but he wasn't sure that he could spread the gospel the way these men could.

Barney leaned toward the stranger, his face soaked with sweat, a vein popping from his neck, his eyes like those of an overmedicated doll—all pupil and without color. "Aargh!" he screamed, "The damn crickets! The goddamn crickets are at it again. They had shut up down by me, but now they are chirping again, the noise is getting to me, Frenchman... the goddamn crickets won't shut up." Barney balled his hands tightly and put them to each temple in frustration.

The stranger stared at Barney and then looked to the Frenchman for some silent counsel and advice.

Slowly, Barney began to relax. He felt emotionally drained and tired from the overwhelming heat and alcohol. He looked down at the four dogs who looked back up at him, unified in their silence. He thought it was time to leave, time to go home with the dogs one more time. Not wanting to be a boor, he extended his hand to the stranger to wish him well and say goodbye.

"You staying much longer?" Barney squinted at the afternoon sun whose rays were now directly in his line of sight.

"Leaving tomorrow." The stranger nodded his head slightly as he spoke. For some reason, this gesture of affirmation seemed to be an appropriate way to close this encounter with Barney.

Barney also nodded to the stranger. Then, he turned his attention to the Frenchman. "Give me my bottle opener, you Alsatian piece of garbage."

"Don't have it."

"You said that you did."

"I lied. I left it in your kitchen last week. The cabinet right next to the sink."

"I should come over there and break you in two, but I am too tired. The sun seems to be setting on me, and me and the dogs got to walk all the way home. I'll get you next week."

Barney whistled and the dogs paired up as they were when they arrived. They didn't wait for Barney. They began the long walk home.

Barney tossed his empty beer bottle to the Frenchman, gave a slight wave, and began to follow the dogs as they walked down the path from the Frenchman's house.

• • •

Barney and the dogs got home as the last shadows of dusk touched his house and barn. Barney pulled the screen door open violently and the dogs scurried in before it closed on them. Tired from the long walk, the dogs collapsed on the beige rope rug that sat in the middle of the room. Barney sat on the red armchair that he'd owned forever; it was his most comfortable piece of furniture.

The sound of Patsy Cline singing "Crazy" came from the darkness that was Barney's bedroom. Barney left his radio on all day and all night. He never opened the blinds in his bedroom because he thought that music sounded better in the dark, or coming from the darkness. He closed his eyes for a moment and tilted his head back on his easy chair. It hadn't been an easy day. Then he remembered.

"'The cabinet right next to the sink…'—that's where the SOB put the damn bottle opener? Well, let's see about that." He popped out of his chair, rushed to the kitchen, opened the cabinet — and there it was! The damn Frenchman had put it in the damn cabinet just like he said. Barney tossed the opener back in the cabinet and slammed the door. "Well, that's another day wasted!!" he shouted to no one.

He came out of the kitchen and looked at the dogs and all save Helen looked back at him. Then, in unison, their heads returned to their resting place on the floor.

It was dark out now. Barney opened the screen door and looked out at the fields that faced his small porch. It was still quite warm and the crickets could be heard chirping in the woods. Barney looked at the dark blue sky, dotted with a million stars and, for a moment, appreciated the beauty of all that surrounded his rather rundown shack in the middle of nowhere (as he so often described it).

He went back into his house and put the latch on the screen door. Tonight it was so damn hot, he would leave the front door open. He looked at the dogs lying on the floor at odd angles. "Worn out by all that walking today, I reckon. They'll sleep well tonight."

Barney took off his sweat-soaked flannel shirt and threw it in the corner of his cabin. He took off his jeans, folded them neatly and placed them over the red chair. He walked into the darkness of his bedroom to go to sleep. Leon Russell was singing "I'm so lonesome I could cry" to the darkness.

As Barney's eyes got used to the darkness, he could see the plastic radio that played all day. It was an ivory-colored radio, with angled vents over the speaker. The vents looked like a sergeant's chevrons placed upside down. Those chevrons were covered with plastic steel. The sound was a bit tinny, but it suited Barney perfectly.

Barney then saw his reflection in the mirror beside his closet. His undershirt was pulled in a number of different ways; it looked like it didn't fit him very well. His underwear was baggy and bunched, located too far away from knobby knees that seemed out of his sync with the rest of his body. Barney reached for the lamp that sat atop his dresser and turned on the light. The vision he saw in the mirror did not improve with the addition of light and definition. On top of that, the light forced him to see the pictures he always left in the darkness with the music.

On top of the dresser, in a room where no one went, in the darkness with the music, was a series of seven pictures of different women, all different ages, all perfectly framed and lined up in a perfect row. They didn't seem to be related to each other. They didn't seem to be related to Barney, but there they sat as a testimony to stories of a bygone age. Each a Kodachrome reminder to Barney of what was, what might have been, and what never will be.

Barney picked up each picture, stared at the subject, and gently stroked the frame as if he were touching each woman one more time. He did not know any of them anymore. They did not know him. After returning the seventh picture to its spot on the dresser, Barney held his forehead, wiped his eyes, and moved his hand from temple to chin repeatedly.

He spoke to each picture individually and collectively when he said, "You'd think that after apologizing for so many things to so many people so many times that I would be pretty good at it. I don't seem to get any better at any of this….Maybe I never really meant it then. Maybe I really mean it now. Maybe I never got better cause I never meant it. I did. Maybe you didn't hear it cause you didn't care either." Barney turned off the light and lay on his bed. It was time for sleep. The radio continued to play as Barney began to snore.

Harpo sat bolt upright from his spot on the rug. He barked twice, as he did every night. Two of the other dogs moved to sleep beside him. Hoppy grabbed Whoever by the scruff of the neck and brought him to his place in line. The dogs slept as they always did, every night, with each other.

In the Frenchman's cabin, the subject of Barney was what kept two men up very late discussing a man and a life. No one heard them speak. It was very hot outside and the crickets were chirping up a storm.

The End

Jack Mulqueen was a hard-drinking Irishman whose face had been scarred by many burly steelworkers from Allentown, Pennsylvania. He had taken the long, slow back road from bars and alleys to this heavyweight championship bout. He had become something of a golden boy lately.

Jack was the people's choice. He was a rising star. His wife was model-pretty, a follower of all the latest trends. She read *People* magazine and knew the stars of every sitcom on TV.

Mulqueen nervously boxed a circle in the large, square ring that was washed white by the high-powered overhead spots. He waited for Carney to enter. His eyes glowed. His body was sweating profusely in the steamy cigar smoke of the Forum. He jabbed at molecules suspended in air, like a babe hitting a mobile in his crib. Mulqueen was ready to take Carney out.

Patrick Carney lay on the trainer's table. He was also sweating profusely. His eyes darted around the room as he sat up on the table. He saw the usual hangers-on with their plastic smiles and empty words of encouragement. He had made them rich—what else would they say? He brushed some sweat from his upper lip and spit into a bucket that had been placed at his feet.

This was to be his fourteenth defense of the heavyweight crown. It seemed like he had held the crown forever. No one could remember the man he beat for the title. He spit in the bucket again. All of the fluid that he had poured into his body in the past weeks was out of his body now. He tried to spit again. There was nothing left. He hopped off the table and jabbed the air.

"We've let that sonofabitch wait long enough. Gimme my robe and let's get this over with."

A member of his entourage draped a velvet blue robe over the champion's shoulders and patted him twice for luck. Various shouts and words of encouragement came from all in the room. Carney wiped his lip one more time and danced out the doorway.

The crowd sat in anticipation of the fight of the century. There was a certain electricity in the air. Everyone in the crowd spoke to each other about "the buzz, the electricity, the excitement" that this match had brought to the arena that night. It was a feeling so palpable that all in attendance spoke about this match with terms of hyperbole. For some reason, tonight was not just going to be another boxing match—something more was at stake.

Everyone was drenched with sweat. Programs were wrapped in tightly turned circles. Cigars were chomped on, not smoked. Pipe stems were breaking. Beer was being consumed at an alarming rate. Some of the most beautiful women in the world were draped over fat men with sunglasses and well-proportioned friends. The speech of the patrons was two beats quicker as they tried to maintain the pace of the atmosphere. Tonight only two men could match that pace, and one of them was sure to falter. The Forum was the place to be.

Carney finally danced into the sight of the crowd. A deafening roar filled the Forum as he slowly jogged the last aisle that went from his dressing room to the ring. A towel was draped over his head. He was eyeing the floor. Carney thought of the million times he had wandered into a bar, slapped a few hundred down, and said that he could lick any man in the world. No one ever challenged him. He'd buy the bar some drinks, tell a few tales, and then move to another bar in another town. He loved to cruise the bars like that.

He was on top of the world. He hated Mulqueen for trying to take all that away from him. He wanted to kill Mulqueen. He wanted to punch him silly. His trainer separated the ropes and Patrick Carney skipped through. He was the "Heavyweight Champeen of the

World," and the cheers of the crowd made sure that he didn't forget it.

Mulqueen eyed Carney with disdain. He hated what he saw. He had given up drinking for this bout, and he had not been seen anywhere but in the gym. He had one shot at Carney, and he did not want to blow it. Carney was known for his ability to slip a punch.

Carney looked across the ring at Mulqueen and chuckled at him. He had seen that look of hatred countless times before. Tough looks from tough men never defeated him, and he knew it. He chuckled to himself. He thought that all these challengers were the same. The steely-eyed look of absolute hatred made Patrick Carney feel better. He knew where he stood now. He was confident.

The excitement of the crowd had reached a fever pitch as the bell rang to begin round one. Mulqueen looked around once, for a moment. He wondered what he was doing in the ring with Carney. Carney ignored the din; it was the background music to slaughter. He cut across the ring to begin to manicure Mulqueen's features.

The fight progressed at a fever pitch. It became evident that these were two fighters who knew their abilities. Carney jabbed incessantly, repeatedly landing on Mulqueen's face. Mulqueen landed occasionally but had trouble because Carney always found a way to dance out of trouble. Still, no matter how many times Carney hit Mulqueen, no damage was done. Carney was scoring points that he did not want. He began to take chances, looking for a knockout punch. Mulqueen held up well. The roar of the crowd had not died since the opening bell.

It was in the fourteenth round that Carney made his boldest move. He tried to circle round Mulqueen just as Mulqueen decided to deliver his Sunday punch. Carney walked right into the punch with eyes wide in amazement. In the split second before the punch landed, he wondered why he had moved that way.

The punch that Mulqueen threw was an atomic blast in Carney's face. Carney's eyes rolled backward, his legs turned to jelly and he fell in the ropes behind him. The ref was between the fighters now. He moved Mulqueen to a neutral corner. Blood was pouring out of Carney's shattered nose and down his chest as he sat half-dazed while the ref began the count. Carney's tongue flapped out of his mouth, and saliva poured over the ring. He fell to his side as the ref counted "six" and lay in a puddle of blood, sweat and saliva.

He heard a bell and great cheers. It was the Toomey fight—the night he had won the championship. His cornermen hoisted him onto their shoulders and out of the ring. What a night! The doc patched him up in the dressing room. He felt the awful sting of the antiseptic as it was applied to his face. It all seemed so real. He lay on the trainer's table and went to sleep.

The End • 37

He dreamt about Alice and how happy she was for him when he won. She had never seen him lose. She had witnessed minor setbacks, but Carney never lost. She was a great gal. She was a woman who'd follow Carney anywhere, but he'd only take her to the classiest joints.

He dreamt about Bogey, Bugsy, and Jake and all the boys from the E Street Y. They always razzed Carney as he was on his way up, but they loved him like a brother. All the sportswriters entered his dreams next, the guys who described his accomplishments in such heroic terms. Carney was neither as good nor as bad as they described him, and he knew it. He thought about the look in every contender's face after he had beaten them. It was a strange look, each contender trying to show Carney that he had not beat them completely. They always tried to toughen up their beaten faces and say, "Good fight, Champ." Carney always smiled and winked at them. He knew their words were empty.

He began to roll around slightly as his dreams came to an end. The locker room was empty and silent. He sat up on the table and felt the tape and plaster that covered half of his face. He blinked his eyes to remove the sleepiness that had overcome him. He looked at his trainer, "Doc," who was the only one left in the room. Doc's eyes were swollen and red. He still had a bloodstained towel draped around his shoulders.

"Hey, Doc, where is everybody? Where's the party? Have I been asleep that long?" The blood had returned to Carney's face.

"You've been out a long time, kid. I was starting to worry about you. The doctor just left a minute ago."

"Oooh, yeah. That Mulqueen was a tough one. He did get me that one time late in the fight. Whoo—that was a close one, huh?"

"Yeah. I thought you were dead, kid. The doctor did a helluva job on you."

Carney started to get dressed. He always showered at home after a championship fight. It was one of his pet superstitions.

"Yeah, well, I guess I'll see you at the party later, huh, Doc?" Carney was getting ready to leave. "I tell you, though, I don't remember the end of this fight. I must be getting old. I don't know how I beat ole Mulqueen. I guess you'll tell me all about it later, though, huh, Doc? Right now, the champeen of all the world has got to get showered and go out on the town. Right, Doc?"

Doc wiped his face with the bloodstained towel. "Go ahead home, champ. I'll talk to you later." He threw the towel into a shower stall and walked into his office.

As Carney left his dressing room, he ran into Mulqueen and a few of his friends on their way out of the arena. They were a lot happier than Carney expected. When they saw him, they all became a little more subdued.

Mulqueen approached Carney and held out his hand. "Good fight, Champ." Mulqueen smiled slightly.

A little startled, Carney shook Mulqueen's hand, smiled and winked at him. Mulqueen and his pals moved on. Carney was scared.

In all the times he had defended his crown, he had never seen a look like that. It almost looked as if Mulqueen had felt sorry for Carney. Carney wanted to rush in and talk to Doc about it, but he thought better of that idea. He stood alone for a moment in the hall between the big arena and the locker room. The place smelled like stale beer and smoked-out cigars. Patrick Carney decided it was time to walk home—alone.

Cellulite Becomes Her

Jim Taylor sat in the coffee bar looking at the greasy fluid that seemed to be floating atop his cup of Green Mountain mocha, the beverage with which he had decided to start his day. As he stared at the Styrofoam cup adorned with scenes of faux nature in tan and yellow upon the green background of the cup, he supported his head with his left hand, his elbow on the coffee bar, periodically wiping his face from his temples to his chin, returning his hand to his forehead—his point of support.

It was 5 a.m. The ornate lobby of the hotel was vacant except for one man in a white tuxedo, bow tie untied, shirt open a few buttons, with hair disheveled. He was sitting at the off-white (Jim wondered if it was ivory) piano playing a slow song that Jim did not recognize. The song had the tempo of a man playing at 5 a.m. yesterday. It was a slow song, tired, and very sad. The man at the piano was playing an "anthem for 5AM"; a tribute to those alone and lonely. A song so perfect for the moment that, as Jim listened, he decided the only thing "inappropriate" that could happen this morning would be if the man in the tuxedo decided to stop.

Single notes, in sequence, without flourish. One note linked to the note before, further linked to the note after. It was a haunting piece made for the inhabitants of the world who moved about a city at 5 a.m. Jim rubbed his face again and looked out at the city streets in front of the hotel coffee bar. It was still dark outside.

Maybe the man in the tuxedo was right—yesterday and last night still lingered; today had not yet started. How many times, how many hotels, how many days did he begin that were still last night? How often was he alone? The piano player had struck an important chord within Jim. Rather than gearing up for the day that he was always forced to begin, Jim focused on the night—the empty streets in large cities that he loved so much. The structures he'd drive by at 5 a.m., still lit from the night before, resembling gems glistening in an oddly constructed pile. Different cities, different lights, differently arranged piles on a hillside or in a notch, whole city blocks quietly illuminated for no one to see. The lights were silent reminders that a vibrant life still existed in the darkness and the night. The lights kept evil at bay. In darkness, evil could rule; the lights were the symbols of a vigilant people rejecting what evil had to offer.

Suddenly, a large panel truck drove directly in front of the coffee bar window and two large packs of papers exploded onto the sidewalk with such a loud noise that Jim was shaken from his reverie. At the same time, the man in the white tuxedo slammed the cover of the piano keyboard closed and shouted "I suck" to no one in particular. He stormed past the doors that opened to the coffee bar toward a destination unknown to Jim.

Jim wanted to stop him. He wanted to tell him that he didn't suck, he was really quite good and that Jim wished he would continue playing. He didn't move from his seat at the bar, though. Doing something like that seemed too weird for his sensibilities. He'd never do something like that; following through on his thoughts was never listed among Jim's strengths.

Jim was further surprised when the young woman behind the coffee bar said, "What's up with that guy? Seems a bit high-strung to me."

Jim had forgotten she was there. He looked at her for a moment, decided his reaction time was too slow and said nothing. She continued to stock the various shelves of the bar preparing for the busy day. She looked tired already. Her workday had begun over an hour ago.

Jim watched her as she worked. She wore a beige wool turtleneck and matching beige pants, which were very tight on her. Over all, she wore a navy blue apron that had two tie strings, which she tied in the front. The apron extended down to her knees. As she moved to different parts of the coffee bar, Jim could see her shoes. They were dark brown with very round tips and appeared to be made out of felt (although Jim doubted this could be possible).

The woman moved with an exquisitely choreographed efficiency. She had obviously held this job for some time, and she was very good at what she did. She was pretty enough. She had a pleasant face whose focal point was the brown tortoiseshell glasses she wore. Jim wasn't appreciating the "woman" before him, though. He was admiring her machine-like efficiency as she completed the tasks of her job. It made him realize that, though he had also been doing the same job for thirty years, he was not nearly as efficient as this woman. As a matter of fact, the more he thought about it, the more he realized that he always did the same tasks differently to avoid ennui.

The problem with "ennui avoidance" is that one risks losing a sense of mastery of one's work or one's life. Jim felt he had mastered nothing. He was a lonely loser wandering through life. Where was that piano player when you needed him? Jim paused to think about how it was that he had grown to be so out of touch with everything he touched. He took a sip of the greasy coffee that resided in his decorator Styrofoam cup. It had gone cold. Jim tossed a dollar on the counter to tip the efficient coffee lady, straightened his tie, and headed for the hotel lobby.

Jim felt for his eyeglass case in the breast pocket of his suit. There was nothing there. He would have to return to his room to get his glasses before he could start his day.

As he walked by the registration desk, a very short woman with jet-black hair smiled. "Good morning, sir. How are you today?"

Jim smiled back at her and attempted to read the name on the tag, which sat at a forty-five-degree angle across her left breast. It was too small to read, though, so he just smiled and said, "Hello."

Annoyed at himself for leaving his glasses in his room, he took the moment to mentally transfer his annoyance to the pleasant woman behind the desk.

"Paid to say 'hello,' paid to be pleasant, probably attends classes on how to smile at anyone at 5 a.m.," Jim mentally grumbled as the elevator doors closed. He considered his reflection in the mirrored doors before him.

He felt ancient. Sometimes he thought that he looked ancient. Mentally, he had retained much of the fire of his youth. That didn't matter, though. Fire didn't hold water in the world in which Jim lived; everyone needed to agree about everything, and controversial thoughts were verboten. To most everyone he encountered, he was old and crazy. Or just old. Or just crazy. No one cared a whit about who Jim was.

The elevator doors opened and Jim walked down the hallway to his room. He let the door fly open as he grabbed his glasses case off the night table and flew out of the room before the door had a chance to close. For whatever reason, Jim was starting his day at full-bore annoyance level. It was going to be difficult to come down from this.

Jim flew past the registration desk and avoided eye contact with the lady of false smiles. He launched himself into the stationary revolving door with such force that he was onto the sidewalk in a second. He strode to his car, which was parked on the street, and drove away with a tire squeal too loud for his age. He was driving to the first of five meetings he was to have that day and didn't want to be late.

• • •

Mindy Callaway was going to be late for work again. She pulled her rust-colored wool turtleneck over her head as she raced toward the bathroom to apply her makeup. She paused for a moment to look at herself as she applied the makeup.

Mindy believed that beauty was still contained within her face, though hidden more deeply than it was when she was young. Today she was jowlier than she would like. Still, contained within the slight face flab and minor wrinkles was a beauty she believed that someone would appreciate someday. It was the beauty that got her through life's challenges because she always felt that people are generally more forgiving of good-looking people than they are of those who are less attractive. Unfortunately, it was also her beauty that got her married twice. She blamed the second divorce on the jowls (her husband left her for a much younger woman). Her eyes teared a bit as she fastened and straightened the auburn wig upon her head. She had been through a lot in her life, and she was proud of herself. Once her wig was in place, she reminded herself that she was running late and it was time to go.

Mindy started her car and drove downtown. She ran the sunglasses kiosk at the local hotel, and the management always scolded her if she opened late. She drove faster than usual so that she might arrive on time. Traffic was building and she slammed her steering wheel in frustration. She could not be late again. Parking was fortuitously available, and she got to the lobby of the hotel just in time.

As she unlocked the wooden sides of the kiosk, she waved hello to Susan behind the registration desk. Susan was kind and always had a big smile for everyone she saw. Mindy felt bad for Susan because she was a single mom who always worked the very early shift (which was generally very busy) so she could be home when her kids got home from school. Susan's mom would get them off to school, but Susan had to be home when they returned, take care of all their needs, and get them to bed just to wake up before dawn and smile sweetly at EVERYONE, whether they were kind to her or not.

Despite all of the challenges that Mindy faced in her own life, she still felt a greater sympathy for Susan.

Mindy was perched on her chair waiting for customers when Susan stopped by to say hello during her morning break.

"How is the sunglasses business, honey? Looks a little slow today."

"Doin' all right, Susan. Would help if the sun were out, though. I always do more business when the sun shines."

"You were almost late again today. Ken was loading up to yell at you, when you walked in and started settin' up. I was going to take him to the office to distract him if I didn't see you comin' in."

"Thanks, dear. Sometimes it's hard for me to get up in the morning—you know. I feel nauseated and it's hard to get goin'."

"I know. I know. My aunt went through what you've been goin' through—it's awful."

"Well, I gotta do it—you know? Sometimes I wonder why. How are the kids?" Mindy always tried to deflect whenever this subject came up.

"Dana made the honor roll—I am so proud of her. Trevor is still struggling. I think kids bully him a bit because of those big, thick glasses, you know?"

"That's great about Dana. I wish I could help with Trevor's glasses, but that's the way it's gotta be for him—with his condition and all."

"I know you tried, you were a big help!"

"Well, I have been in glasses all my life. Started out in NYC with regular eyeglasses for all kinds of people, now I sell these things to people who buy stuff in hotel lobbies."

Susan tried to be upbeat because she sensed Mindy beginning to waver. She seemed a bit sad to Susan. "Well…you are the best, honey. The absolute best."

Mindy smiled at Susan and looked down at the floor. "I had a friend, she was joking I think, that said I moved from real glasses to sunglasses because I couldn't stand looking at the world clearly any-more—because of all that happened and all." Mindy's voice trailed off a bit as she finished her sentence. She couldn't help but think that her friend was kind of right. What was she doing in this hotel lobby anyway?

Susan tapped her arm as she moved back toward the desk. "Don't you worry, girl—you're just fine. You're a good soul. And if you weren't here, you wouldn't know me! How would that be?" Susan smiled broadly at Mindy. "Gotta go now, break time is over. Time to make the doughnuts!"

Mindy smiled a thin smile of recognition at Susan. She always ended their conversations that way. Mindy was upset and was barely able to say, "See you later" as Susan departed.

The rest of Mindy's day went pretty much as any other. A few old creepy men would flirt with her as they feigned an interest in glasses. Some older women would shop and try on glasses for what seemed to be an interminable amount of time and then ask Mindy to show them the cheapest pair that she had. Susan would wave as she departed, and her replacement, Kurt, would not acknowledge Mindy's presence in any way as he made his way to the registration desk.

Mindy was just about to close up the kiosk when a strange man came flying though the revolving door, saw her kiosk, and shouted, "Sunglasses! Just what I need. I've been torturing myself all day without them. Please, please don't close up. I am in desperate need of your sunglasses."

Mindy turned and smiled in the general direction of the man who had caused the outburst. That kind of energy was not usually displayed in a staid hotel lobby, and she found it to be both charming and entertaining.

With a strangely reassuring voice, she calmly told the agitated man that she was not going anywhere. She would wait for him.

The man allowed his gait to slow and his manner to relax as he approached the kiosk. He saw something very appealing in Mindy's face and manner, and he did not want to upset her with boorish behavior.

He hesitated a bit as he approached Mindy to describe what he needed. The strength of the emotion he was feeling had become physical, and he was almost jittery with excitement as he spoke to Mindy. Women did not usually have such a profound effect on him.

"See these?" He took his glasses off and handed them to Mindy. "I think I need those crazy flip-down, old man, should-be-in-an-asylum type things that one attaches to glasses to convert them to sunglasses. Do you have them? I need them desperately."

Mindy's hand touched the stranger's as he handed her his glasses. The intensity of feeling she felt was palpable. She got excited by touching him. A physical feeling overtook her frame and made her tremble slightly while trying to locate the glasses he needed.

She found what she thought he needed and passed them to him in a manner that was almost shy. Their hands touched again, and she looked up at his face and saw that he was looking right into her eyes.

"How are these?" The words barely broke the plane of her lips.

The man smiled at her and flipped the glasses over in his left hand, pretending to examine them. "These are.... They are just perfect. I'll take them."

"Don't you want to know what they cost?" The old women had conditioned Mindy well over the years.

"Whatever," the man said absentmindedly. "I need them. I'll take them." He handed the glasses back to Mindy to bag. Their hands touched again, and Mindy thought that he had done it on purpose that time. She felt a certain distance develop between her brain and her eyes. It was as if she were watching the transaction as it was taking place. She felt the trembling. Her eyes teared as she wrapped up the glasses for the stranger.

The man cleared his throat. "My name is Jim. I am just passing through town on business, but I will be here a couple more days. You gotta know..." Jim was feeling nervous now. Maybe this was all a huge mistake. "You gotta know that I don't normally do this."

He now had Mindy's attention, but his nervousness had also engaged Mindy's sense of humor, which she generally brought out to deflect or "paper over" intense feelings, intense discussions. "You mean buy sunglasses?" She smiled slyly as she spoke.

"No… No…" Jim put his hands before him as if this movement could stop the conversation and allow him to restart on his terms. He looked into Mindy's eyes again and sighed.

Mindy thought he looked almost desperate, mentally begging her for the permission to speak, to finish what he had begun. She smiled again and said, "Sorry…go ahead."

"Well," Jim stammered again. "I don't want you to think I'm some sort of weirdo, but I'd like to ask you to dinner tonight."

Mindy had finished bagging the glasses, and she handed them to him as she spoke. Privately, she was thrilled—the psychic tension between the two of them was a feeling that she did not want to ignore. She also felt a true weirdo would not allow the possibility of his being a weirdo by describing himself as a potential weirdo, so she thought it was probably safe. Besides, it was just dinner, they'd be in a public place, and she could escape if she needed to.

"My name is Mindy." She shook his hand and smiled as she spoke. "I would love to eat dinner with you tonight. I'd like to have some time to go home and freshen up. How about we meet here in the lobby at around 7:30?"

"Mindy, perfect. Yes, Mindy, that would be great." Jim was obviously so thrilled that she had agreed that he fell into nervous speech patterns that usually showed themselves at times of extreme joy or stress. "Seven thirty, right here. I'll see you later." He raced toward the elevator feeling better than he had felt in quite some time.

Mindy smiled at what she thought was an almost boyish enthusiasm in the man she had just met, boarded up the kiosk, and walked swiftly toward her car to go home and change. She was keenly excited about the prospect of dinner with this man, and she was not quite sure why.

Jim Taylor was happier than he had been in years. He could not believe he had made a date for dinner. This woman was good looking, and she seemed kind of funny. The fact that she was pretty, the fact that she seemed funny, were secondary to Jim because there was definitely some kind of sexual tension between them. He felt it. The feeling was as intense as anything he had ever felt.

There was only one other time in his life that he felt anything approaching the feeling he had with Mindy. There was a female employee in a fashion optical place on 23rd Street in Manhattan. Back in the '80's, she had helped him decide on glasses, then he saw her again when he picked them up. Both times, high feelings, tense muscles, stammering—just like today. He remembered that she also showed him pictures of herself with her family. She was trembling, too. It was incredible, but he had been engaged to another woman at the time and he never acted on it. Never forgot the feeling, but never acted on it. He wondered about how many other times he might have seen her, how many times he might have run into her. They worked in the same area after all. The woman he was engaged to was out of his life fast; the woman he had this feeling for never got in. He shook his head at the irony as the elevator doors opened, and he went to his room.

As Mindy drove home, her mind was consumed by so many thoughts. What should she wear? What will she talk about? How awkward might this date be? It had been a very long time since her last date, and she felt like a kid again. A young woman starting over.

She unlocked the door to her apartment, stripped quickly, and jumped into the shower. Obviously, there were some things that she was not going to discuss this evening. She hoped she could hold up her end of the conversation.

Out of the shower, she considered her body in the mirror. "Thicker than I used to be, less curves and more straight lines of skin where curves used to be."

She sighed. "I am what I am…it's only dinner, after all."

Jim put on the TV in his hotel room and went to the bathroom to shower. While he was showering, he wondered what he would talk about, how he could engage this woman in interesting conversation. He spent his entire life speaking with strangers, but this process of involving himself with someone new put more fear into him. He didn't know what to say.

He put on his suit and prepared to meet Mindy in the lobby. Should he get her flowers or something like that? Too hokey. A present might seem too forward or cause her to assume intentions he didn't want her to think he had, though he definitely had those intentions. How could he break the ice in a charming way that might get her to feel the sense of attraction he had for her? He saw the bedtime mints on his pillow and the mints from last night on the table beside his bed. He had a plan.

Mindy decided she was going to wear her favorite dress to dinner tonight. The dress was midnight blue and extended just below her knees—very "age appropriate," she thought. The dress also had buttons down the front that extended from her neck to below her breasts. She put the dress on and unbuttoned the top two buttons. She smiled at her reflection in the mirror. She felt pretty. She knew she looked pretty. She sprayed herself with her favorite perfume and fastened her wig upon her head. Perhaps she was not as sculpted as she used to be, but she did look pretty tonight. She felt proud. She felt sexy. She opened the third button of her dress to reveal more of her chest. Very "sex appropriate," she thought as she smiled at her reflection and left her apartment to return to the hotel. She hummed as she walked to her car. The sounds of her high heels hitting the ground made her want to stride, not walk. She was filled with confidence. Her spirits were as high as they had ever been. She parked her car and walked into the hotel.

Kurt looked up from his station behind the front desk but barely acknowledged her existence. He was generally not interested in women and definitely not interested in a woman who sold sunglasses in the lobby of "his hotel." Derek, the concierge, gave her a wink and a lighthearted wave as she walked past him. Mindy considered this wordless high praise from Derek, and it made her feel even better. Her red lips were glistening, her eyes were alive with a feeling of great anticipation. She smiled broadly and gave what she felt to be a coquettish wave to Jim, who was leaning against the table reserved for the house phone, his arms crossed in front of him.

Jim removed his hand from his right biceps and did a solitary hand-waving motion to Mindy in response to her wave. She looked so happy, he couldn't help but smile at her as she approached.

With his left hand, he reached for Mindy's right hand and brought it to his lips to kiss. Mindy almost squealed with girlish excitement as he kissed her hand. It was a perfect way for him to greet her.

"So glad you could come. And right on time. I love punctuality in a woman."

"Thank you, Jim. You are so tres elegant; that was a greeting that could fill a girl's head." Mindy couldn't stop smiling. She couldn't stop her body from trembling. It had been such a long, long time since she had had feelings like these. She stared straight into Jim's eyes as they spoke.

Jim was excited and concerned that the same feelings of trembling anticipation had returned to the pit of his stomach. He didn't want Mindy to know how excited he was, and yet he couldn't wait to share the feeling, and he couldn't explain any of these emotions in any rational way. These feelings were just occurring, and he had no control over their onset or intensity.

He looked at Mindy's face and then surreptitiously surveyed her body. She must have been gorgeous when she was younger. Jim noticed that this was not a chiseled woman embodying the freshly cut appearance of youth who stood before him. Veins were visible over some of the bones of her hands. What had once been sculpted body lines had grown into each other. Some curves had probably squared off some, and the length of her dress likely hid some cellulite. But at this time and in this moment no one could possibly feel more attractive to Jim than Mindy. As he thought all these things, he realized that he might be staring at her, and he rushed to ask a question.

"Dinner...where would you like to eat?" Jim clapped his hands together as he spoke.

Mindy had not stopped smiling. Of course, she caught Jim sizing up her dress and her body. She hoped that he approved. The fact that he was looking at her as a woman was not insulting; in fact, she was further titillated by his interest. For a moment the depressed realist within her wished she had spent more time at the gym lately, wished she could simply rub the age spots off of her hands, wished she could tighten up the lines on her face. She shook herself out of this reverie quickly.

"Dinner... Yes... Where? Honestly, I had not given it much thought at all. This was all so sudden. I work here but I don't often eat out around here, so I'm not sure where we should go. What do you like?"

For a moment the lounge lizard within almost had Jim saying "you," but he resisted for the high road and answered her question. "I usually eat at the hotel when I am in town. That might not be great for you since you work here and all... I don't know..."

Mindy did not want to be a bother. "The hotel is fine," she blurted out. "Let's eat here."

Jim was a bit taken aback by her outburst, but he was happy to oblige, and they were seated at a window table in the hotel's finest restaurant. When they first sat down, there was an awkward silence that Jim decided to break.

As the busboy filled their water glasses, Jim spoke. "I wanted you to know how important this date is to me. I want to make a good first impression with you. I thought of buying flowers, but I didn't and now I am sorry that I didn't."

Mindy reached her hand across the table to interrupt Jim. Tenderly she told him, "There was no need to do that…"

Jim was intent on finishing his thought. "Yes, thank you, I am sure you are right, but I didn't want to arrive empty-handed." He reached into his pocket and pulled out four bedtime mints that were on his pillow and in his room. "I want you to have these. I stole them for you." He put the mints on the plate before Mindy.

Mindy leaned back in her chair and covered her mouth with her left hand as she laughed. She was now completely smitten. This man obviously was sensitive while having a sense of humor that she could enjoy.

"Thank you. Thank you so much for thinking of me when committing misdemeanors. The funny thing is that I have a whole bag of those in my hut outside in the lobby. Susan, the girl who works the early morning shift, gives them to me all the time. I told her I enjoyed them once and now I have a lifetime supply. But…" she reached across to touch his hand again as she spoke, "THESE will be SPECIAL MINTS TO

ME. I'll never eat these because I will always want to remember where they came from. They will be a reminder of this night forever." She smiled and winked at Jim as she continued to massage his hand with hers.

The icebreaker had worked better than he ever expected. Jim felt that a real connection was developing. He was as happy as he'd ever been. The conversation began to flow as they spoke about where they had been and what they had done in their lives. Jim was convinced that they must have run into each other before because they both worked on the same block in New York City at the same time. Still, he couldn't imagine meeting her and not seeing in their youth what he was seeing that night. So maybe they never had met before. Maybe they weren't ready to meet each other then and they were ready now. His mind was racing with all manner of alternatives as they spoke about all sorts of things. Jim was so excited about this connection that he didn't notice that Mindy was tiring as the dinner went on.

The meal had been finished and the coffee complete when Jim looked at Mindy and saw the crow's-feet at the corners of her eyes, the skin that was somewhat drooping around the corners of her mouth, and the small pockets of flab around her biceps— she was magnificent! This was not a woman he would have dated in his youth, but this is a woman that he would never leave today. "I could walk the streets of this town till dawn with you. Let's do it. You'd be held lightly in my arms, and we will speak about whatever comes to mind. It will be great!"

Mindy was exhausted, but she didn't want Jim to know. She was caught up in the reverie and excitement of the evening, too. Still, she knew it was time she got to sleep. She had stretched way beyond her limit for Jim. She was feeling nauseated. She had to go home. She would be a mess tomorrow if she didn't. She felt like she was going to cry as she spoke.

"Jim, there is nothing I'd rather do tonight than walk the streets talking with you. I can't, I just can't. I am so exhausted, and I have to get up early in the morning. I hate to say it, but I really think that I have to go home."

Jim was crestfallen, and it showed on his face. "But, but the night is so young and we're having so much fun! How about we just walk till midnight then?" Jim smiled, attempting to flirt his way into a few more hours with Mindy. It was a strategy he had worked successfully before with other women at other bars in other towns.

Mindy began to tear up a bit. She really didn't want to leave. She considered telling Jim about her problem, but it was way too early to do so. There'd be more time for that. At least she hoped they'd have more time together. Still, Mindy did not want to lie.

"I feel a bit ill. Maybe do this again tomorrow? More dinner? More conversation then?"

"Problem with the fish you ate?" Jim needed an explanation for this unanticipated turn of events.

"Yes, maybe the fish.... I really need to go." Mindy's condition was deteriorating quickly.

"Tomorrow then. I will be traveling, but I should arrive back here around 6. Could we meet around 7:30 again? Maybe more dinner, but a different locale and no more fish!" Jim smiled as he spoke and raised his voice when speaking about the fish for faux emphasis.

Mindy smiled and held Jim's hand as they got up to leave. She felt the excitement she had felt early in the day as they walked together toward her car. Mindy was exhausted and felt very ill. She was afraid that Jim might move to kiss her good night, and she couldn't possibly bring herself to do it. Fortunately, he held the car door for her as she got in.

Jim took one last look at Mindy. He found it exciting that her dress hiked up to the middle of her thigh as she sat in the car. "You in?" As Mindy nodded in the affirmative, he simply said "Tomorrow" as he closed the door.

Mindy waved and drove off as Jim stood in the street alone and watched her. He never thought that he'd ever find any particular attractiveness in a car's directional signal, but he smiled and waved again as Mindy's car turned and drove away. The street was empty again, and Jim slowly surveyed the situation that surrounded him. Large empty office buildings, small empty stores and restaurants, parked empty cars surrounded him on the street, yet he had never felt so happy, so filled with life before. Jim had experienced enough special days and special nights in his life to know that he had just experienced another. A day that began with a disturbed man playing an ode to the night before ended with Jim alone in the city finding happiness in the directional signal of a combustion engine driven by someone he did not know twelve hours before.

Jim clapped his hands and let out a hoot. "I love this town," he said to no one in particular. He returned to the hotel entrance and whistled as he approached the elevator that took him to his floor. He knew he would have trouble sleeping this night, and he had to get up early in the morning.

Mindy drove home as quickly as she could. Once inside her apartment, she tore off her dress and fell to her hands and knees, retching as she made her way to the bathroom. She vomited once on the floor, grasped for the toilet bowl, and vomited violently again. She tried to push herself up to a standing position, but she felt too weak to move. Finally, after some time had passed, and with great effort, she pulled herself up and looked in the mirror.

Her wig was crooked and perched at an odd angle across her flushed face. She looked at her half-naked reflection and sighed. Her hands gripped the counter to keep her from falling to the floor. She was exhausted and miserable, and these feelings were exacerbated by the great joy she had felt no more than two hours before. She set herself to clean the vomit off the floor (it seemed like this was the 1,000th time), and then she would shower and try to sleep.

As Mindy climbed into the shower, she slipped and grabbed the towel rack to prevent her fall. Once in the hot shower, she began to soap her whole body and rinse, when all of what she was experiencing took control of her psyche and overwhelmed her. She sat down in the tub and began to weep uncontrollably. She wept for so many reasons, she couldn't determine which one drove her to actually start. She just knew that she was very sick and very sad. "Why me?" She cried as she threw her soap at the bathroom wall. "Why now? Why now?"

She wondered why she would have the luck to find a man like Jim at a time like this. She wondered what she had ever done that was so evil that she deserved this fate. After a period of time, she collected herself and turned off the water.

She sat in the shower dripping and naked. Her head was resting upon her folded arms, which were resting upon her knees that were bent before her. She started to tear up as she sat and remembered how wonderful her night had been. Finally, she reached for a towel, dried herself off and went to bed. Physically, she had felt better after she had vomited. There was a trace of fatalistic resignation in her smile as she thought to herself, "It wasn't the fish!"

Jim had had a fitful night's sleep. Afraid that he would not wake up to his alarm, he instead woke up every hour until the alarm sounded. When the clock finally buzzed to wake him, he rolled out of bed half asleep and exhausted. Still, he had not lost the exuberance he felt the evening before. Once showered and dressed, he felt a newfound purposefulness, happy to know that today would end at least as well as last night did. He would see Mindy again tonight. He smiled as he slipped the complimentary shower cap and half-used tube of hotel shampoo into his jacket pocket. He tapped the door before him as he headed toward the lobby. Today would be a good day.

The doors to the elevator opened and the "fresh flowers of the day," a bouquet of pink and white roses, extended from the depths of the plain black vase that held them. Something about the roses struck Jim in a curious way. He admired them for a moment and surveyed the hotel lobby for "the authorities." Seeing that no one was paying attention to the solitary man who had just stepped from the empty elevator, Jim quickly reached for and removed a white rose from the vase. The thorn of the rose pricked his finger as he grasped it, but the pain was of no consequence. Jim had to make it to Mindy's sunglass hut without being seen. With great speed and superior stealth, Jim made it to the sunglass hut and deposited the white flower, the shower cap, and the half-used tube of shampoo on the top of the hut. He then raced to the coffee shop to order some Green Mountain mocha and cover his tracks.

With his caper complete, Jim enjoyed the coffee more today than he had yesterday. The same efficient woman was performing similar tasks flawlessly, but Jim found more enjoyment in everything he did and experienced today. For a fleeting moment, he noticed the ivory piano and wondered what had happened to the man who played so well for no one. He deposited the dollar bill on the bar and left the hotel to find his car and begin another day.

Mindy awoke with a start and sat bolt upright in her bed. "My God, I am late again! Ken is going to kill me." Feeling dizzy, she twirled her body to the side of her bed and looked at her clock again. It was 5:37, not 7:35 as she had thought at first. She had almost another two hours of sleep due her and her now rapidly fluttering heart. "Never should have gotten rid of those clocks with two hands…. These digital things are a nightmare for the 'midnight dyslexic' like me."

She put her head back on the pillow, pulled the covers over her naked body, and tried to find a way to time an uninterrupted ninety minutes of pure, deep sleep. This mission was never accomplished; she woke up three more times before it was time to get up and get ready for work.

As she dressed, Mindy thought about Jim and the night before. She had such a wonderful time. He seemed like he was such a wonderful guy. Why was he alone? Was he alone? Oh my God, how could she have never thought about that? She was so caught up in dreams of romance and love that she never considered the alternative.

For a moment she stopped all that she was doing and looked at the bathroom mirror. Love? How did that word find its way into her thought patterns? Love? After a couple of goddamn hours? Impossible but intriguing in its possibility. She thought it would be fun to confront Jim with this concept tonight. She had a plan. It might be fun to scare the heck out of him. Mindy smiled at the person she saw in the mirror before her. "You go, girl." She touched the face of her reflected image with her toothbrush, then set it on the sink and departed for work.

Mindy entered the lobby of the hotel and smiled at Susan, who was helping a customer. As she approached the sunglasses hut, she saw that something seemed to be on top of the cart. Mindy sighed. After hotel functions, and around the holidays, she often found half-consumed beverages littered around the kiosk. It always annoyed her. She thought it was gross. Why should she have to clean up someone else's party mess? As she got closer, she saw it was not a glass at all. She reached up and pulled down the white rose, the shower cap, and the partially used tube of shampoo.

For a second, she wondered who would leave such things on the hut, and then she realized that all were "hotel issue" (though she had no idea where the rose came from). She smiled at each item as she took a moment to consider each individually. First she held them close to her heart. She then kissed them each individually and tucked them away into her bag—hidden from the authorities.

Mindy was a hopeless romantic. She spent most of her free time that day thinking of Jim and wondering where they would go and what they would do that night. When Susan came over to say hello, Mindy told her about Jim.

Susan smiled as she saw both joy and excitement embodied in Mindy's face. Still, she admonished her friend to temper her expectations. "Beware the traveling salesman, my dear. The man in town for just a few nights is usually just in town for one or two nights. You get what I am sayin'?"

Mindy would have none of it. "I know, I know, but this is different. The feelings are real. The excitement is genuine. I tremble when I am around him! That has never happened to me ever, ever." Mindy clapped her hands for emphasis and let them fall in her lap. She knew that she'd been around for too long to fall into some sort of schoolgirl crush.

Susan wanted to be positive, but she was still suspicious. "Does he know everything about you? Did you share this rather big thing you've been dealing with lately with him?"

For a moment Mindy became quiet, almost sullen. "Well… no…"

Susan began to roll her eyes. Mindy saw this and tried to cut her short. "It's too early. Give me a chance. Maybe tonight." Mindy began to bite her thumbnail. "Maybe tonight."

"True love doesn't run away, Mindy. You tell him. You tell him soon. I couldn't bear to see you hurt."

Mindy tenderly reached for Susan's forearm to touch her, to reassure her, to let her know that she appreciated her friend's concern. She smiled and a certain sadness of resignation seemed to appear on what was a truly cheerful face.

"You are a good friend, Susan. You really are." She got off her chair and hugged her friend for emphasis. Susan seemed touched by this action and brushed a phantom tear away from the corner of her eye as she smiled at Mindy.

"You WILL have a good time tonight, girl! You will! You deserve it." Susan smiled as she walked back to the front desk.

For a few minutes, Mindy considered her conversation with Susan and thought about what she should do next. Seven thirty couldn't come fast enough for her today.

At about five o'clock, Mindy closed down the hut and hurried home to get ready for her evening with Jim. Tonight she decided to be alluring. She showered when she got home and opted for her low-cut green and white striped dress that was formfitting to the waist and then was flowing to below the knee.

Complemented with white heels, panty hose, and her favorite (most expensive) perfume, she felt as though she was "quite a dish." As she approached her car and began to get in, she wondered when she last felt so young and attractive. It was a long, long time ago. The nervous feeling she had in the pit of her stomach began to show itself as she left her apartment; it reached a crescendo as she parked at the hotel.

A feeling of irrational panic hit her as she placed her hand on the door to the hotel. Was she overdressed? They hadn't been specific. She didn't know where they were going. Why hadn't she set some guidelines with Jim the night before? She bit her bottom lip, sighed audibly and entered the hotel lobby.

Fortunately, she saw Jim as soon as she entered. He was leaning against the wall by the hut, and he was wearing a suit. Extreme relief replaced panic as Mindy's feeling of the moment.

Jim had spent his day moving from one client site to another, thinking of Mindy and their evening together in between visits. He had received a restaurant recommendation from a client he trusted, and he could not wait to take Mindy there. The amount of excitement he felt as he drove around the area that day surprised Jim. He didn't think it was possible to feel this way again. Most of his life had been spent in situations surreal. His was an engaging personality that attracted too few friends. He felt that all that he had experienced, all that was different in his life, was sufficient reward for the sentence of solitary confinement he had handed himself. To be in a small cell with no hope of human contact was one thing, one could almost rationalize the existence, the punishment for prior bad behavior. To have the entire world at one's fingertips and the resources to experience a big portion of it only to realize that his was an existence in solitude seemed particularly pernicious. Jim's life was the embodiment of "cruel and unusual" punishment. This was not to say that Jim never shared a laugh or a good time with anyone. The problem he had was that all happiness and laughter was transient. All that was meaningless was permanent. Jim had spent his life following his nose around the world and reached the point where he realized that it was all just one damn thing after another.

Mindy was different, though. There was something that felt very real about her. The physical feelings she inspired in Jim were unprecedented in his life. The joy that they shared in each other's company was invigorating. Jim felt that they had developed a portolan chart to the perfect relationship—how did that happen?

Jim's car strayed from the road and woke him from his reverie about Mindy. Jim thought as if he were speaking to another human being. "I know it's only one night…but what a night. Why is she alone? Why doesn't she have anyone?" He thought back to the graffiti he had read on a restroom wall in New

Orleans many years before: "No matter how beautiful she is, no matter how much she laughs at your jokes and tells you how great you are, no matter how perfect she seems…someone, somewhere is sick of her shit." This graffiti had informed many of Jim's thoughts on relationships, and he smiled and shook his head as it came to the front of his thought process one more time.

"Not her…she's different. Why is she alone?" As Jim drove, cynicism battled romance for control of his addled brain. In the end, his only conclusion was that "he'd see what would happen" that night.

As he drew nearer to the hotel, he thought more about the impact Mindy was having on his life. He struggled to understand the relationship. For some reason, the girl in the optical shop came to mind. It was so long ago, so far away. That was the only other time he had felt anything like the feelings he had for Mindy today. She worked in New York City. She worked in an optical shop. Is there any way this could be the same person? How cool would that be? Jim had another subject for conversation that evening. He was going to pin this down. Maybe it's her…. How cool would that be?

Jim parked his car in the hotel garage and waved to the woman who smiled to everyone (he didn't know her as "Susan") as he strode through the lobby to get to his room and freshen himself up before his "date." Jim laughed at the description. He was also beginning to feel great anticipation at the prospect of seeing Mindy again.

He pushed his hotel door open with a flourish and tossed his business bag onto his bed with reckless abandon. Then he thought better of it and took the bag off the bed. "You never know how this date may end, big boy." Jim spoke out loud to no one in particular. He laughed at himself for even considering the possibility of a sexual ending to his dinner with Mindy.

Jim washed himself and did a minor splash of cologne across areas of his body that Mindy could conceivably smell at dinner.

He looked at himself in the mirror and winked. He thought he looked pretty good tonight. He slapped his hands, left his room and positioned himself against his favorite wall in the lobby to await Mindy's arrival.

Jim was struck by how confident and how beautiful Mindy looked as she walked across the lobby to meet him. Her face seemed to light up when she saw him, and she gave him a big wave and smile as she approached. Jim pretended he did not know to whom it was she was waving and looked behind him for some other suspect. Mindy rolled her eyes and laughed. When she reached Jim, she put her arm around his neck and planted a large kiss on his cheek as an old couple shuffled by and nodded their approval.

Jim looked nonplussed. "Excuse me, do I know you?"

Mindy playfully slapped his arm and said, "I am so happy to see you. I've been excited about this date all day!" Mindy's eyes moistened as she spoke, and it seemed that some being borne of excitement was going to burst out of her frame as she spoke.

Jim was pleasantly surprised by the enthusiasm of Mindy's greeting. He couldn't remember ever being greeted with such enthusiasm before. He reached around Mindy's waist and pulled her close to him. Hugging her tightly, he whispered, "You have no idea how much I've looked forward to this moment."

Silently Mindy squealed with delight. The night was beginning perfectly.

Jim paused to look in Mindy's eyes. "Are you OK? Looked like you didn't feel too well when you left last night. Was the fish that bad?"

Lost in the reverie of the day was the realism of the evening's sickness. In some ways, it had become such a common occurrence that Mindy thought it not strange. Still, it was an abrupt ending to the evening which had been going so well. She hadn't thought about concocting an excuse, "Yes, about last night…"

Jim sensed that something serious was about to come out of Mindy's mouth, and he didn't want the evening to begin with something heavy. He reached into his pocket and pulled out a small, plastic shoehorn that he had stolen from his room.

"I got this for you." Jim held the shoehorn like a single stem flower before him. "I hope that you like it."

Mindy smiled, grasped the shoehorn with both hands, and placed it by her lips as she spoke. "So beautiful, so useful, so stolen. I will treasure this special gift for the rest of my days." She held the shoehorn upon her breast and gently kissed Jim's cheek; this time there was a deeper, more serious emotion attached to this otherwise innocuous kiss. Mindy's eyes engaged Jim's and held them for a moment before bowing to the frivolity of the situation.

"It's like dating John Dillinger. I treasure all that you steal for me." Mindy smiled at Jim. The silliness of the situation was pushed aside by a deep feeling that was growing within her. This was a special man to Mindy, and she knew it.

Privately, she was happy that Jim had changed the subject from the night before. She was not yet ready to share all that she needed to share with Jim. There would be time for that.

So caught up were they in the joy they felt in being with each other that they forgot they were in a hotel lobby and began to converse and engage each other in the pleasantries of their day.

After a few minutes, Mindy's attention was finally diverted away from Jim's face to notice the sunglass hut nearby—closed for business.

She looked at Jim and said: "You know what happened to me today? Some freak left a collection of garbage on my hut last night, and I had to clean it up before I could open up."

Crestfallen but maintaining a level of nonchalance that belied his feelings, he inquired, "Garbage? On the hut? That's weird. Who would do such a thing? What did they leave?"

Smiling inside, Mindy continued, "Happens all the time, thoughtless drunks leave all manner of crap on the hut and I have to clean it. It really bugs me. This time it was used—*used*, mind you—shampoo, a shower cap, and a flower. What kind of weirdo carries that crap around? I tossed it all and then opened the hut."

Jim was feeling very low, but he could not let on. How could she not associate his playfulness with this weirdness? How could she miss the point? Maybe she wasn't as great as he thought. He had to move on before she saw any sign of emotion from him.

Jim clapped his hands together. "Well, here we are standing and chatting in a hotel lobby when we could be sitting and enjoying a nice dinner together. What say we go get something to eat? You hungry? I know a place…"

Looking at the sheepish man before her almost made Mindy regret her little joke at Jim's expense. She would fix it—later. For now, she agreed with Jim. It was time to leave the hotel lobby and find something to eat.

"You are so right, my friend, let's eat. Lead on—I will follow." She took her left arm and hooked herself into the crook of Jim's right elbow. Then she brushed her body against his. "Let's eat, Jim…. Where are we going?"

Still trying to overcome what he was classifying as his childish disappointment with Mindy, Jim took control of himself and the situation. "You and I are going to a very special place. Follow me." Arm in arm, they walked out of the lobby of the hotel.

Not far from the hotel entrance stood a small community theater that once was a venue for many poorly acted plays. The stage was elevated about four feet off the floor, and large ornate columns covered with random hand-carved masks framed the stage. When arranged for full seating, the theater could hold approximately 200 patrons of the local arts. Often, it was less than half full, and eventually the theater closed. For a while, the building lay fallow waiting for others to repurpose its beauty. A wealthy banker and his pretentious wife—who viewed herself as a baroness of some long lost, tiny duchy—decided that this venue would be the perfect setting for a community opera house. They bought the building and added color to the black walls and hand-carved columns. Bright white combined with bright blue and green were splashed upon the walls. Some of the hand-carved masks were painted also. There were fun frescoes commissioned by the wife, who loved to spend money. She hired an artist from New York to "embody the seasons" with the frescoes, and surprisingly the art was quite good. The theater adopted a new elegance that was appreciated by the Brahmans of this small town. Preposterously, they began an opera season where overdressed people would pay too much to pretend to enjoy some poorly sung operas. This foray into high art had lasted for a little more than three years before this theater shut its doors and turned out its lights again. The "baroness" died while selecting opera glasses for a season that was not to be.

Without a benefactress, the building fell into disrepair. About three years earlier a young, entre-preneurial chef decided to buy the building and convert it into a restaurant. The fact that the building had outlasted its prior two tenants and that nothing that went on here survived very long did not concern the young restaurateur. In fact, he embraced the history and called his restaurant "The Opera House." He painted the stanchions that supported the stage black and strategically aimed the blue and red spotlights around the restaurant. Other than that, he left the walls and columns of the opera house exactly as they had stood so many years before. The cacophony of colors created the eclectic appearance of the venue and lent a certain romance to the dining experience. You could be seated beside a fine art fresco or a painted wood carving. Your table could be bathed in red or blue spotlight or be lit by a single long taper in the darkness. The tablecloths and chairs were black, the napkins deep red. Viewed from a distance and with the right perspective, it appeared as if the guests and their food were suspended in the ether, a location so special that something important was bound to happen to any who had decided to stop there to eat.

As they sat at their table, a table bathed in deep blue light, Jim was finishing the story of the history of the building and restaurant.

Mindy was still absorbing the eerie beauty of the surroundings as Jim spoke. This place rekindled the physical feeling she had felt in her first encounter with Jim. She was trembling with excitement and extreme sexual tension as she tried to compose herself to speak.

She turned her head once more to look at the odd art and the colored wood carvings. She folded her hands beneath her chin and stared into Jim's eyes as she spoke.

"And to think, all this time I thought that this was just an opera house." She smiled as she grasped Jim's hand. "I've got to get out more, I guess…. Who knew?" Then she paused to look at their hands that were now clasped together and back into Jim's eyes. "How did you ever find this place? You don't even live here."

Jim looked shy, almost sheepish, as he spoke. Mindy thought that something might be bothering him. "A client…a client told me about it." Jim looked at the napkin on the table before him as he spoke. He loved this place and wanted Mindy to love it also. He was uncomfortable because he couldn't tell if she liked it or not. Finally, he just blurted out, "Well, do you like it?"

Mindy released his hand and looked nonplussed for a moment. "Like it? You mean this place? Like it? I LOVE IT. It is absolutely perfect. Perfectly decorated and oooh so romantic!!" She slapped his hand playfully as she spoke.

Feeling relieved, Jim smiled at Mindy and opened his menu. Mindy stopped him by placing her right hand at the top of the menu and pushing it down toward his lap. Her eyes seemed to glisten as she spoke, "What do you do for a living anyway?"

Jim was surprised they had not spoken of it before. He thought his work boring, and he felt that there would always be time to speak of the mundane. He didn't want to lose the special feeling he had for Mindy. "I work for the government. I travel a lot, know a lot of people. One of my clients recommended this place to me. He told me it was a good place to go for a fine romantic evening."

Mindy's eyes widened and her smile broadened. "Are we about to have a 'fine romantic evening'??!!! Really!! This work you do for the government—sounds very secretive, very illegal."

Jim shook his head, "No, no. Not that. It's just, well…"

Mindy put a single finger on Jim's lips to silence him. "There will be time for all that talk."

Jim was somewhat relieved that he didn't need to go further.

"Does the government ask you to steal for a living?"

"What?" Jim was very confused. "What? No… why would you ask?" Jim's response was interrupted by Mindy reaching into her bag to reveal a shower cap, a half-used tube of shampoo, and a white rose that was beginning to wilt with the remains of the day.

"Care to explain yourself, Mr. Dillinger?" Mindy held the rose beneath her nose and attempted to smell the sweet smell that had long since died. The shocked look on Jim's face told Mindy she had done well. Jim was blubbering as he spoke.

"You said it was junk. You said you threw it all away!"

Mindy smiled and extended her hand to clasp Jim's. "I never said that I threw it away."

The dinner proceeded as their relationship had started—an endless series of conversations about small culture, trivial icons, or memories of times past and the way things were.

Jim told the story of the optical store a few times more. They were both pretty convinced they had met before. They were both pretty convinced they had had that same feeling of sexual tension (which they were now more comfortable discussing). They both wished they had acted then. How can we ignore such strong emotions? How could they have dismissed what could have been a utopian future for the immediate mediocrity? That's life.

"Let's love what we have now." Mindy exhorted Jim to leave the past behind. "Let's create our future together."

Mindy had been holding Jim's hand as they spoke and gripped him more tightly now for emphasis. She was willing to release herself to him. She wanted them to break the bonds of the uniquely personal to share a unique existence together.

Jim looked into Mindy's eyes and nodded in agreement. "I asked my boss today for next month off and he said OK. I plan to come back here and spend all my time with you. I do have one question, though. How did this happen?"

Mindy smiled and looked at Jim again. "I don't know how and I don't know why. But I do know this: Your voice, your thought, your humor speaks to me in a way that no other does. I want to hold it dear to me as I do today, forever. However long that may be." Mindy's voice began to trail off a bit here. She decided that now was the time to share her full story with Jim. It wouldn't be easy, but he deserved it. She began to speak again when a loud buzzing sound began to emanate from beneath Jim's sports jacket.

"Oh shit," he exclaimed. Jim pulled the device out and stared at the screen before him. "Oh shit," he said again. There was a visible sadness etched into the corner of his eyes as he looked at Mindy's face. "I am so sorry. It's from the boss. Some kind of emergency. I have to contact him immediately. I have to go. I'm so sorry." Jim was stammering.

Mindy saw how sad and serious Jim looked and felt bad for him. "I understand. It's OK. We'll see each other tomorrow. Right?" Mindy was trying to be understanding even though she was completely confused and concerned.

Jim was already absent and distracted; it must have been something very important. "Yes Mindy…of course…6 p.m. tomorrow by the hut. I am so sorry. I will walk you to your car."

Back in his room, Jim called his boss and argued loud and long about the assignment he'd been given. "Not now, not this, I deserve the chance to say no!" He slammed the phone back into its cradle without uttering another word. He slammed his fist onto the faux mahogany desk so hard that it shook the nondescript painting of purple clouds surrounding a red mountain that rose out of a bluish turquoise sea. Jim looked at the painting that slammed into the wall; a name plate on the bottom of the frame read "Bali Hai." "Really," he said to no one. "Bali Hai?"

He tried to open a door, which could not be opened no matter how hard he turned the knob. He thought the door led to a balcony where he envisioned himself able to think about the cruel circumstances of the evening. Faux door to faux patio, a faux picture of Bali Hai hanging over a faux mahogany desk—was anything real in this hotel?

He returned to the chair before the desk and picture. He had to get in touch with Mindy, and he had no idea how it could be done.

He took a slice of paper out of the faux leather folio on the desk and began to write his explanation to Mindy. He told her that it was an emergency. He told her it could be a while before he returned. He gave her his phone number and asked that she call him with hers. He told her how much he cared and how much he looked forward to seeing her again. He sealed the letter in the envelope provided by the hotel. How would he get the note to Mindy? He sat alone on the edge of the bed and thought about how best to get it to her. He slapped his hands as he thought of the perfect plan. He went to the elevator and grabbed a white rose from the faux Grecian urn. He rode to the lobby and placed the white rose atop the note and placed both upon the top of the sunglass hut. He kissed his hand and touched the note and the rose before he left. He returned to his room, packed his things, and left the hotel without further hesitation, just as his boss had directed him to do.

Later that evening, a group of very inebriated college students staggered into the hotel lobby. They found great humor in banging into furniture and other things that were not funny. They saw the sunglass hut and decided it would be great fun to try to break into the hut and get free glasses. They shook, they prodded, and they jimmied the hut without success, laughing at every moment. A note and a rose fell down from the top of the hut and lay on the floor as the hotel manager came from behind the desk to break up their reverie. One young lad, overcome with too much alcohol and the fear of being prosecuted, vomited all that he had eaten all over the floor. The rose and the note were soiled beyond recognition. One of the janitors came to clean the mess and remove the collateral damage.

The next day Mindy came to the hut hoping to find out what happened to Jim. But there was no note, no sign of him. That night she waited until 7 for him to return, but he did not come. Not knowing Jim's last name, she couldn't find him in any directory. She asked Susan to check the hotel registry, but the entry said "US Government–Department of the Interior" without any other identifying information. Mindy was crestfallen and didn't know what to do. Days became weeks and she did not hear from Jim.

Jim had been away for some time, and he wondered why Mindy never called. He tried calling the hotel a few times but was curtly cut off by a man named Kurt who had a Northern European accent. Kurt would always remind Jim "that he was not a messenger for any man."

Finally, his task completed, his boss satisfied, Jim drove back to the hotel to rekindle his relationship with Mindy. His excitement grew as he drew closer. In the hotel lobby one afternoon he looked for Mindy and her sunglasses hut. The hut was still there, but it was closed. Jim was confused. It was mid-afternoon, where could she be?

"Excuse, excuse me," Jim put on a faux smile to put the woman of faux smiles at ease. "I am looking for the woman who manages the sunglasses hut. Her name is Mindy. Mindy Callaway. Do you know where she might be?"

The woman behind the counter stopped what she was doing to survey Jim's countenance. "It's you…. You're the guy. The one Mindy liked so well. You didn't even leave a note. I don't think you want to be speaking with me right now. I don't know that I can control what I'd like to say to you."

Jim had no idea what was going on or what this woman was talking about. As the woman stared at Jim, her face of anger melted into streams of tears that began to flow from the corners of 'her eyes. She tried to harden herself to be mean to Jim, but her sadness overwhelmed her.

"She's…she's gone. She had been struggling with the cancer, and it just became too much for her." The sentences were coming out of this woman's mouth intermittently between long sobs and tears. "You were her hope, and when you left without a trace, she lost all hope. The treatments beat her down badly. She had no one. I tried to help her, but it wasn't enough, I guess." The woman was crying uncontrollably.

"But I left her a note with a rose on top of the hut. I always left things for her there."

The woman behind the desk had regained control of herself and wiped the tears from the side of her face. "She didn't get no note. She thought you just up and left and that you didn't care."

"Cancer? She never mentioned that." Jim didn't know what news to react to. He didn't realize how little he knew and how much of an impact he had had on Mindy. "Couldn't she?" "How?" Jim couldn't even finish a thought or a sentence. He didn't know what to do. Mumbling to himself, he left the woman behind the desk to wander the streets of the city and process what he had just learned.

After an evening of thinking and drinking and wandering the streets of the city speaking to himself, Jim returned to the lobby of the hotel planning to go to sleep. He saw an ivory piano in a room by the door as he entered the lobby.

Half drunk and emotionally exhausted, Jim stood before the piano and began to play an absentminded collection of notes to help focus his thoughts. He was playing a song about yesterday, not about tomorrow. He played about love lost and the darkest part of his existence. The loneliest part of life when one realizes he is witnessing his own demise and discovering his own irrelevance, which others had realized all along. It was a song for the inner darkness of the revelation of the empty self to what had been a busy, but not worthy existence. It was a song to selfishness and doubt, to braggadocio and insecurity. It was a song of longing for love and its connections in an uncaring and vapid existence. It was an ode to sadness and disappointment, opportunities squandered, life wasted and spent. It was a plea for a "do over" in a game that can't be redone. It was a plaintive cry to yesterday to inform a better tomorrow. It was sung to Mindy, who was his last shot at redemption, and in Jim's mind it fell completely short. Finally, in a fit of complete frustration and exasperation, Jim slammed the cover of the keyboard shut and screamed "I suck" to no one in particular. He stormed past the coffee shop doors, toward his room to lead what he believed would be a continuation of his meaningless existence. He had become a prisoner—under sentence of death.

A man in a suit was seated at the coffee bar as Jim stormed by. He smiled at the woman in the beige turtleneck who had served him his coffee. "I kind of wish that guy kept playing; it all sounded pretty good to me. I didn't think that he sucked."

Without hesitation the woman continued to work at the tasks before her as she spoke, "Seems a bit high-strung to me."

Easter Sunday in the Suburbs

Palm Sunday has a certain peacefulness to it. To those who would notice, the celebration of a triumphant entry into a small village long ago is lived as a day subdued. A quiet peacefulness falls over the world, a noticeable lack of celebration highlighted by a muffled calm, an intense peacefulness that can never be discerned on any other day. Though the Sunday changes from year to year, the feeling of Palm Sunday can always be perceived; one just has to care enough to notice.

Easter Sunday is quite different than Palm Sunday due to its colorful flamboyance. Easter has become a self-conscious celebration of the narcissistic nature of God's least perfect creation. On a holiday that celebrates rebirth and glory, potential and the power of faith, a frilly insignificance rules the day.

Little John Carter was almost always bored at church. Being only five, he was dragged to church every Sunday by his parents. His father would never allow him to play any games. He could not wave to his friends or speak out loud. Church was a place of too many rules for him.

On this particular Sunday, his parents forced him to wear his fancy clothes. These clothes itched him all over, and he didn't like to wear them. His mother told him he looked so cute and took his picture before Mass. His father told him it was a special day. Before the family left for church, John saw a big chocolate bunny and candy on the kitchen counter. He hoped he could have some of that after church. He always looked forward to candy.

John's mom wore a pretty light blue dress that day. She looked very beautiful. John had never seen her wear a fancy hat before. It covered one of her eyes and sometimes made it hard for her to see things. She had bumped into two different chairs at home before they left for church.

John's dad wore the kind of clothes he always wore to work, so he didn't look very different. Dad called what he wore a suit. Lots of men wore suits to church that day.

As the family walked from their car to the church, John Carter looked at all the people in all of their fancy clothes and colorful dresses. Maybe church will be different today, he thought. Everyone sure did get dressed up. Maybe it wouldn't be as boring as usual.

As they approached the front door, John noticed someone who looked different from the others. She didn't walk so well and she was leaning on a cane.

She didn't have nice clothes like everyone else. Her clothes looked old, but not as old as she.

The woman wore a grey knitted cap over her matted hair. She didn't have many teeth left, and the ones that remained were a noticeable presence in her mouth. She shuffled rather than walked, and her eyes were shot red. At the entrance, she ran into another lady she seemed to know.

"New cane, Gladys? That's a nice one."

The lady with the skullcap replied, "Mo left it to me. Called it his 'staff' he did. You know Mo, he was always that way. Anyway, I figured I might as well use it—it being Easter and all. You know what I mean?" Gladys laughed a toothless laugh. John thought she looked gross.

He heard his mom whisper to his dad, "Shoot me if I ever become that way. Oh my God…look at Mary Ellen. How did she ever squeeze herself into that dress? There are the Proctors, remember to be nice if we have to stop to speak with them. She is new to the club and she has a very big mouth." John's dad nodded in silence. He and John Carter followed his wife to the same pew where they always sat. John Carter squirmed slightly as he squeezed between his parents. They wanted him to sit down, but he got up on his knees and watched as all the people came into the church. He loved the colorful clothes.

John Carter smiled when he saw Mrs. Carrier walk through the door. She wore a very short bright red dress and very high-heeled shoes. She seemed to be looking for someone as she came into church. All of a sudden, she stopped and smiled very sweetly. John Carter saw Mr. Jacobs wave to her. He was smiling, too. Then Mr. Carrier came behind her and touched her back, and she stopped smiling as they went to sit down. When he tried to hold her hand, she pulled it away. John Carter thought something had made her sad or angry.

Then the Willard family came into church. They were good friends with Mom and Dad. Seeing them made John Carter happy. Mrs. Willard wore a dress that had flowers all over it. The flowers were all different colors. The dress was very tight, and she wore high heels that made her look very tall. No one in their family said anything to each other, and they sat far apart in the pew. It was as if they were waiting for more people to fill in the gaps between them.

John Carter was getting tired of looking at all the people, no matter how colorful they were. His knees also hurt. He turned around and put his head on his mother's lap and began to drift toward sleep. The adults could handle this Easter stuff; he wanted to go to sleep.

As John lay sleeping, more parishioners filled the church. Melanie sat at the edge of a pew—alone again. She wore her favorite grey dress that no one ever knew about because no one knew her. She knew she wasn't beautiful, but she was not hideously ugly. She sat and wondered why she could never catch and hold a man. She watched as woman after woman entered the church wearing fancy clothing and expensive jewelry, hanging on to the arm of an obviously successful man, and yet she knew no one. No one loved her. She saw Allison Burroughs with her dyed red hair, large-bellied body, and multilayered makeup enter the church with her husband—a well-groomed businessman who was reasonably good looking. How did that happen? What did that woman ever do to deserve him? Allison was one of many that Melanie watched enter church that day. She envied all of them.

As the congregation grew, a young family approached the Willards' row and asked if they could squeeze together so that the young family could sit down. This was difficult for the Willards to do, but common courtesy required it. The process of moving them together was a slow one as they each squeezed the space of family dysfunction from between them. They grimaced, rolled their eyes, and scooted slowly, but eventually they were together in the pew and the young family was able to sit down.

The Good family entered church just before the service began. Jeannie Good was wearing a peacock blue dress with matching heels and hat. Jim was wearing the suit that he was married in. Last Easter, they were the happiest couple in the congregation as they had just recently been married. They had fallen in love the previous Easter while holding hands during the Lord's Prayer. When the prayer was over, Jim did not let go of Jeannie's hand. He would say that he felt the electrical energy between them as they held hands that day. He took her to breakfast after that Mass, they made love that afternoon, and they were married as soon as their divorces were finalized. This day, Jeannie bit her lip as she entered the church—a nervous habit she had recently developed. Jim yawned and surveyed the congregation. Both had grown fearful that the other was saying the Lord's Prayer with someone else, but neither would broach the subject. Instead, Jim often yawned and Jeannie had learned to bite her lip.

The service was about to begin, so the cantor approached the podium that stood beside the altar to make announcements to the congregation. She was cantor to the parish most every week, and she enjoyed the role of leading the congregation. Today she wore a form-fitting black dress, with a sequined black flower that extended from her left shoulder over her breasts, terminating mid-thigh at her hemline. She realized that black was not a traditional Easter color, but she felt pretty and sexy in this dress, so she wanted to wear it today.

The cantor was overweight, but she was very proud of her appearance. She wore bright red nail polish to contrast with the black. On her left hand, there was a ring of diamonds to further accentuate the ensemble. As she stepped up to the podium, she noticed a small fissure in the floor of the church. She was annoyed that the crack had still not been sealed. She thought it was very dangerous, but the pastor felt it cost too much money to fix and did not really pose a threat to any of the parishioners anyway, so he ignored her.

The pastor was slated to say the Mass that day, and he always required that he be announced before the service could begin. The cantor did as he asked. The congregation smiled as one and looked forward to the homily the pastor would deliver. He was a man who spoke very well.

The pastor was just putting the finishing touches on his vestments when he heard his name announced. Quickly he shuffled the altar servers out the door and got ready for another Easter Mass. Number 21 for him.

The congregation rose and sang the entrance hymn. The service had begun. The priest joined his congregation in prayer. The priest always sealed the church for the reading of the epistle. He felt anyone who arrived that late for Mass should be shamed as an example to the rest of the congregation. He wanted them to open the creaky doors and have the towns-folk all turn as one to see who dared to appear so late. After the alleluia verse, the pastor would say the gospel and his homily. For that, he would open the doors; there was no shame for anyone who came to hear him speak no matter how late they were. Today it would be slightly different.

The doors were sealed shut as the cantor stood on her podium to sing the alleluia verse. As she approached the microphone to sing, Gladys leaned heavily on Mo's' staff to push herself out of her seat. Mrs. Carrier winked at John Jacobs as they stood before their spouses in the house of the Lord. Jeannie Good looked left and John Good looked right as they stood to sing. None of the Willard family looked at anybody as they stood to sing. John Carter's mom could not stand because her son was still asleep in her lap. As the cantor began to sing, the pastor surreptitiously looked at his watch, realizing the Mass was running long. He mentally pledged that he would breeze through his homily.

The cantor held her hands up to lead the congregation in song, and things began to happen. Her red nails grew longer and longer. The ring of diamonds on her left hand glowed, and her figure grew till she seemed to encompass half the altar.

A wave of uncertain uneasiness overcame the congregation. No one could believe that what they were seeing was real. There was just not enough time to process a vision so surreal. At first there were audible gasps, then women and children began to scream. Most were rooted in horror and disbelief, not sure what they should say or do. Dark grey smoke began to emanate from the fissure by the cantor's podium and quickly filled the church. Rows of people rushed the exits screaming in ungodly ways. The cantor, now rising halfway to the ceiling of the church, cracked a black whip of dark fire over the heads of any who tried to leave.

Large black beasts flew from the baptismal font to block the doors. The song of the cantor degenerated into a series of the dark chants of Lucifer sung in tongues long dead. The church was filled with the songs of forgotten tongues celebrating the darkness of evil.

People were screaming in horror, pushing each other aside to find a way to save themselves. Some were trying to find a way to pray in the all-encompassing gloom. The pastor stood for a moment to speak against the demon and then sat back down captivated by fear. The cantor's eyes glowed red, her mouth spewed grey smoke.

Mrs. Carrier ran into the arms of Mr. Jacobs. The black whip swirled around the heads of all in the congregation. The air conditioning units flew out of the walls. Darker, black smoke came from the fissure in the floor. All grew dark as the cantor's face and shape changed continually. Some stood rooted in horror. Many could not stop screaming; most had dropped to the floor in utter despair.

Gladys held Mo's staff aloft and screamed. "Be gone, Satan. This staff can defeat you. So long as this staff is held aloft, you cannot triumph!" Her eyes glowed and all signs of age seemed to fall away from her body. No one in the congregation paid attention to her as the cantor's whip tried to wrap around her cane and wrench it from her hands. She did not falter. The cane remained above her head. The Goods ran from their pew in opposite directions, and the whip cracked before them to stop their advance.

The cantor turned her gaze to Gladys. "Drop the staff!" the guttural voice filled the church.

Gladys took a small step back. She was too terrified to speak. She had no idea why this was so important to do. She shook her head and continued to hold the staff aloft.

The cantor turned her attention to the priest. He sat with his head in his hands crying. He did not know what to do. People fought each other to escape the church, but none could get past the sealed doors. The dark shape on the altar now consumed half the church. Deep laughter now drowned out the terrified screams that filled the hall. Church pews were flying everywhere. Everyone was certain they were going to die and that there could be no salvation. A dark sadness and the overwhelming silence of hopelessness now consumed the group.

• • •

At that moment, John Carter's dad sat down beside his sleeping son and kissed his forehead. John Carter wiped his eyes and looked up at his father, who was smiling down at him.

"I don't like Easter, Daddy," John Carter said. "It's never any fun for me."

"Easter isn't just for you, John Carter. It's for others in the parish, too."

"I guess so, Dad. Let's go have some chocolate."

The father brought his son up to his shoulder and carried him out of the church. On the way out, Mrs. Jacobs stopped to greet the family. She tweaked John Carter on the nose and said, "How is my boy Jimmy doing today? Is this a fun Easter for you?"

Mom always said it was inappropriate for a child to correct an adult when they made a mistake. But Mrs. Jacobs almost always got John Carter's name wrong.

John Carter smiled at Mrs. Jacobs and shook his head. "Yes."

As they headed toward the car, John Carter saw that the priest had just finished changing the words in what he called the "Sunday Sign" outside of church. To John Carter, the "Sunday Sign" was one of the main attractions when he went to church. Dad would always read the "Sunday Sign" to him as they left and try to tell him what the words meant.

"What's the sign say, Daddy? What's the sign say?"

Thirty minutes of sleep, the prospect of chocolate, and a complete "Sunday Sign" had revitalized John Carter.

At that moment, John Carter's dad was saying hello to another parishioner. "What, son? Oh…the sign. The sign says, 'Will the redeemer find faith in the world?'"

"What does that mean, Dad?"

"I don't know, John Carter. I guess we'll find out next week, OK?"

"OK." The son's thoughts had moved on to chocolate bunnies.

• • •

The pastor never repaired the fissure in the tile. That would have cost too much money.

Hannah Sue

Hannah Sue McCarthy was rejoicing in the moment. To the entire world, or at least those present at the Halloween Gala, she was Elizabeth the First; beneath the pouffy skirt and alabaster makeup, the Virgin Queen still lived. She was as happy as she had ever been in her twenty-two years on earth. She was dancing and twirling and reveling in the freedom of being someone else for the evening.

Later, as she stood sipping her punch, Walter, dressed as William Shakespeare, approached her from behind, wrapped his arms around her waist, and began to recite Sonnet 116. "Love is not love that alters when it alteration finds, nor bends with the remover to remove…"

Hannah's eyes glistened as she turned around to smile at him. "If I ever asked you, could you recite the entire sonnet? You are out of your league and out of your time Walter 'Shakespeare' Stone. Her alabaster makeup cracked slightly as she smiled and kissed him on the cheek.

Walter was taken by Hannah's beauty. Her very long, blonde hair was tightly braided with strung pearls, framing her face in a half circle. Her hands were small and her fingertips were slightly pointed. She had a beautiful figure which could be discerned by those who endeavored to see through the multi-layered sixteenth-century garb. One grey eye and one brown eye stared at him tenderly as he looked at her. Stroking his fake mustache and beard, he said, "What's with the different color contacts? Did you research Elizabeth's life and discover that she had one brown eye or something?"

Hannah would not release Walter from her gaze as she considered every contour of his face. "The brown eye is the only bit of Hannah that was allowed to come tonight. I couldn't leave her behind entirely. She would have been terrified." Hannah was still smiling, but she knew that Walter did not realize how much pain she still felt inside.

Walter laughed and pulled Hannah's body close to his. "Where do you come up with these ideas?" He kissed her on the cheek.

"Will…Will Shakespeare…come with us, quick!" A friend beckoned from across the room. "We have much catching up to do and very little time to do it." Reid had just returned from Scotland. To Hannah's eyes, he already appeared to be very drunk. She hoped that Walter would not leave her for very long. Drunk or sober, Reid held a special spell over Walter. In

Hannah's mind, Reid was not always the most positive influence on Walter; they usually found a way of doing something inappropriate together.

Walter paused for a moment, silently requesting approval from Hannah, even though he did not think he needed it. Hannah bade him farewell, told him to have a good time, and reminded him not to forget about her. Hannah watched Walter for a moment as he left her. Unbeknownst to him, hardly noticeable to anyone, she began to chew on the nail of her right thumb. Extreme nervousness overtook her body, and she began to tremble as her eyes darted around the room: Another attack that Hannah described as "anxiety" was taking hold of her.

It had happened before. It was not unusual for her to feel extreme, almost terminal fear at times when she was experiencing great joy—she never told anyone about this because she was certain that others would think her crazy to be feeling this way. To many. the thought that anything and everything was possible brought feelings of great hope and opportunity, particularly when one was happy; for Hannah, it just raised the odds that all that was good was about to crumble, crack, and wither away. A small goodbye at a party would undoubtedly lead to some greater degradation, some awful collapse of a tunnel upon which she had built all hope. She had trouble with any act of separation, she hated the most temporary goodbye, and she always hoped for the happiness that could act as an emotional poultice over the scars that would not heal. Yet, once experienced, that happiness would lead to the inevitable sense of apprehension and great terror that those feelings could end at a moment's notice. She closed her eyes slightly, pursed her lips, and silently said goodbye to Walter one more time even though he was now very far away.

Her feelings of foreboding were exacerbated by the fact that Hannah knew very few people at the party. Even after all these years, she was still fearful of crowds, and as memories of the past started to surface, she could sense the all too familiar feelings of isolation and helplessness take hold of her. As these thoughts entered her mind, she tried to thrust them aside, but she couldn't shake that deeply uncomfortable feeling of being ill at ease and different in a world that was very much the same.

Minutes passed and still Walter had not yet returned. Hannah became more and more agitated. Her eyes were wide as she searched the faces of the party-goers, frantically looking for someone she knew.

Her mind wandered back to that time in the airport. Her mother had taken her brother, her sister, and Hannah to meet their Uncle Ed. He was flying in from Seattle. Hannah was wearing her favorite flowered dress and white Mary Janes in honor of meeting Uncle Ed for the first time. It was also her first time at an airport, and she was both excited and curious. She was the eldest child, so even though she was only four years old, her mother always expected her to be more responsible than the others. They were waiting on line for some fast food (was it McDonald's?) when Hannah Sue got bored and began to wander away from the family. She remembered how her mother turned to scream at her.

"Hannah Sue McCarthy, you get back here!" The tone and volume of her mother's voice let Hannah know how angry she was. "Your Uncle Ed will be here soon. Stay with your brother and sister." Her mother grabbed the plastic tray with their food order and led her children to a table in the corner.

She was busy trying to secure the baby in a high chair when her mother noticed that they did not have any napkins. She told Hannah Sue to go to the counter, get a bunch of napkins, and return straight away, without dawdling.

As Hannah Sue approached the counter, a well-dressed man in a suit came up to her.

"Hannah? Hannah Sue McCarthy?" The man had an odd smile on his face and a slight question in his voice, as if he was not sure it was she.

Hannah nodded slightly. Her mom had always told her never to speak with strangers.

The man with the nice suit smiled very broadly. "It's me, your Uncle Ed." His arms spread wide to embrace her. Hannah smiled and ran to him.

"My mom, my brother, and sister are in the corner waiting for me to bring back napkins. You wanna come?" Hannah was very proud of herself for finding Uncle Ed first.

Uncle Ed smiled as he spoke to her. "Let's go buy some chocolates to surprise everyone first. Then we'll bring the candy and the napkins with us to their table."

Hannah loved chocolate and couldn't wait to surprise her family. She smiled and held Uncle Ed's hand as they ran to buy chocolate together.

It took her family and every law enforcement officer in the state over six weeks to find Hannah. Her shoes were gone and her beautiful flowered dress was torn and soiled beyond recognition. Every day for six weeks, that man made her do things that no four-year-old should do. Every day for six weeks, she cried while he hit her. Every day for six weeks, she tried so hard to be both quiet and brave. Every day for six weeks, she ate peanut butter and jelly sandwiches twice a day, barely surviving, waiting for help to come. She wondered what had happened to her family. She wondered whether her mom would be angry with her. Each day was worse than the day before.

Help finally came. Men with guns and helmets came bursting through the front door of the small, dark house in which she had been imprisoned. Hannah remembered that some of the men who came through the door to save her vomited when they saw her tied to what the man in the suit laughingly called "the spinning wheel." Her naked body was marked with cigarette burns and small knife wounds. The pictures of Hannah that adorned the walls of the room in which she was kept gave her rescuers an all too accurate picture of just how awful her period of captivity had been.

A few of the men who had broken through the door were so angry that they struck the man in the suit with their guns. Blood and teeth were flying from his foul mouth as Hannah was released from her bondage.

Hannah remembered how she cried as the lady police officers wrapped her in blankets and carried her to the ambulance. She remembered how she screamed and recoiled when the medical technicians tried to strap her to the bed in the ambulance. They told Hannah that it was for "her own good," and Hannah became instantly compliant. It was what the man in the suit always said before he strapped her down.

Hannah shook her head and looked around the room to see if anyone at the party could see her crying. She touched the corner of her eyes to make it stop (another trick she had to learn at the hands of the man in the suit) and walked quickly across the dance floor to the ladies room. Hannah needed to touch up her makeup.

She examined her face closely in the bathroom mirror as she reapplied her alabaster foundation. Hannah looked older than she was and felt older than she looked. To Hannah, there were lines on her face that appeared at that moment for the very first time.

She had never noticed them before. She was mentally exhausted.

She remembered how so many people told her so many times that "time heals all wounds," that she would get by "in good time." That "life goes on." The endless platitudes of consolation offered little to her. Those people had not been in the room with that man. They had not been forced to do the things that she did, suffer the way she suffered—these people— how would they, how could they know? Tears of anger and deep, never-ending pain filled her eyes. Hannah was furious, hurt, and in great need for a respite from the agony. Where was Walter?

She was alone in a party of strangers dressed as a sixteenth-century virgin, tired of herself and ex- hausted by the situation. The concept of being a proper girlfriend and waiting alone at a large party was doing her no good at all. She resolved to find her date.

Hannah marched toward the bar in a manner that would have made the forceful Virgin Queen proud. She had a feeling that Walter and Reid would be there. She was not disappointed in her assessment of the situation. She was very disappointed with Walter.

The men sat with a tray of shot glasses, half of which were empty, in front of them and two women, dressed like harlot witches, beside them. Hannah was not amused, but Reid found the whole situation quite humorous.

He smiled as he put his arm around Hannah's shoulder. "These are licensed professionals," he slurred. "Right, girls?"

The two women smiled vacantly.

"Yep." Reid pointed his shot glass in Hannah's general direction as he spoke. "Professional witches they are, Ms. Hannah. Put a spell on us, they did." Reid drank his shot and almost knocked over a bar stool as he stumbled and spoke. "Nothing we could do about it, right, amigo?"

Walter held his very drunk head in his left hand and nodded an affirmative response to his friend's question.

Hannah's eyes were ablaze as she stared at the foursome. She was doing everything she could to contain her rage. "Takes more than a little makeup and a see-through skirt to turn a couple of suburban tarts into harlots, Reid. You might as well continue your dream, though."

"Well, what do you know about hookers anyway, Virgin Queen?" Reid foolishly interjected.

Hannah turned toward Walter. She felt her eyes burning as her makeup ran into them.

"And you! How could you?" She picked up an empty shot glass and hurled it at his head. The glass shattered against the wall.

Hannah lifted the hem of her skirt and stormed out of the party—alone. Walter was too drunk to follow her.

Hannah headed for the sanctuary of her apartment. Her makeup had been almost washed off her face as two wide lines of water extended from her eyes to her chin.

As she walked, she spoke aloud to no one in particular, "Says he'd be right back and he doesn't return. Says he loves me and he ends up drinking shots with his stupid friend and some faceless tarts. Leaves me to fend for myself at some strange party in some strange place. Why did she ask me to get the napkins? Why didn't she get them herself? How did he know my name?"

Hannah stopped on the street and looked at the scar on the back of her hand. She studied the ligature scars that surrounded both wrists. She bit her thumb and watched the world pass by as she stood. "Goddamn it!" she screamed to no one in particular. "Goddamn them! Goddamn him!" She tossed the hem of the skirt which she held in her hand at the ongoing traffic and resumed her march to her only sanctuary. Her mind refused to set her free; the memories returned one more time.

It had taken her mother and father two days to get to the hospital after Hannah had been rescued. They blamed it on the long trip and trouble finding a place to stay. Hannah remembered thinking that her mother's eyes looked different and that her breath smelled funny. Once Hannah returned home, it became obvious to her that she was not the only one in the family to fall victim to the man in the suit.

Her mother drank all the time. Eventually, she shipped the kids to their uncles and aunts because she could not handle looking at them anymore. By the time Hannah was twelve, she had lived with three different sets of relatives. She decided to strike out on her own. She left a note and moved to New York City to become an actress. At the age of twelve, she looked sixteen and had had more life experience than many adults. She thought she could handle it.

Hannah stopped at the traffic light near her apartment and surveyed the streets she used to roam as a teenager. They were empty and lifeless. Tonight, she stood on the corner as the Virgin Queen; how many other times had she stood on the corner as a younger purveyor of something quite different?

It was late, but not very late. Hannah watched as a woman left an apartment two doors down with a baby in a stroller. As they approached, she saw that the child clutched a pale blue stuffed kitty. Thankfully, at that moment, the light changed and Hannah could cross the street. The child, the cat—they both reinforced the thoughts that she was trying to "outwalk" on the streets of the city that night.

She ran to her apartment house and upstairs to the bedroom. She tossed her dress onto her bedroom floor and lay on her bed covers crying uncontrollably.

Her mind was now open to all the awful that she had experienced in her life. After her experience with the "man in the suit," her life became a caricature of what goes for human existence. The drugs, the men, the abortions…it was so sordid and salacious that one could view her existence as a series of panels in an erotic comic strip for losers. The kitty she saw on the street reminded her of a different kitten at a different time. A friend, an abortion, a cat…it started when she was so young, when would the insanity end? Where, when, how, will life go on? Hannah knew that "anxiety" was rearing its unsightly head again.

"Anxiety" was being alone and strapped down again. When she asked the nurse what the straps were for and why she was in the hospital, the nurse told her that the straps were "for her own good" and that she was not yet "clear." These were memories that could not be checked at her apartment door. Her life followed her everywhere she went. She wanted to get away and memory would not let her go. People were always strapping her down "for her own good," and she never felt any better. Hannah felt like she was going to vomit.

• • •

Hannah awakened the following morning emotionally drained from the night before. She sat up and looked around, uncertain about whether or not she should get out of bed.

Her apartment was filled with furniture that had incredibly clean lines to it. There were no intricate pieces, no complex art or crockery. Hannah had learned the value of being utilitarian early in life. Her life away from home had exposed her to enough of the complex; she relished simplicity and elegance in her home. She pushed herself off the bed and into her kitchen. The night had been awful, but she was used to awful nights by now. A cup of tea would do her good.

She filled the blue ceramic pot with water, pulled a teabag out of the cupboard, and placed it in a blue ceramic cup. The teapot whistled and she poured the hot water into her cup.

Hannah examined her body as she sat at the table. She could see the tracks that almost no one ever noticed. She felt the wrinkles at the corners of her eyes and at the edges of her lips that no one ever commented on. Her thighs were flabby, and the muscles in her arms waddled when she was very excited or agitated. Her hair, which had looked so splendid the night before, was damaged; its ends were split. She held a handful of her hair before her eyes and released an audible sigh of frustration.

Then she saw her reflection in the tea and considered where she'd been. How could she ever share the details of her life with anyone? She felt so alone. Could her life ever be normal?

Hannah reached for the kitchen knife that was held in a butcher block on her counter. The blade was wide and very sharp. She dragged it across her breasts, pausing over her heart and exerting some pressure upon the point of the knife. She thought that maybe she should try to draw some blood.

Returning to her reflection in the tea, she pulled the knife up to her throat and wondered what it would feel like and how hard she'd have to cut to find an artery that would kill her quickly. She put the teacup down and, for a moment, placed the knife on the table.

Committed to leaving the world in the state in which she came in, Hannah removed her undergarments and tossed them on the floor. She turned her left arm over and laid it flat on the kitchen table. She picked the knife up again and began to draw it across her wrist. Slowly but surely, she began to exert more and more pressure on the blade.

With a swift decisiveness that she had not exhibited in some time, Hannah picked up the knife and slammed it, point down, into her kitchen table. It stood there wavering for a moment and then clattered sideways onto the table.

Hannah held her head in her hands and began to cry. Tears fell onto the kitchen table and formed small puddles before her. Tears ran off the edge of her nose and down the palms of her hands. Tears ran down her arms and collected in the crooks of her elbows.

Hannah couldn't stop crying. She didn't know how to tell herself that everything would be all right someday. She'd never believed anyone who had said it to her.

How could Walter have abandoned her? How could he become a thoughtless lout at the hands of a mindless brigand like Reid? She punched her kitchen table, and the knife fell off the table and caught, point down, in the cheap linoleum floor that was cracked and worn. Hannah stared at the knife for a moment, and her mind began to return to thoughts of death and suicide when the bell to her apartment rang.

Startled, Hannah wiped the tears from her face and her arms and scooted to the peephole to see who it might be.

An athletic-looking woman with short brown hair was spinning a tennis racket in Hannah's hallway. She wore a white tank top with wide blue stripes down the sides and a pair of tight-fitting shorts. Her attention was diverted by something in the hallway as Hannah watched her.

"Rachel," Hannah mumbled to herself. Hannah had never been so happy to see her. Rachel was Hannah's anchor to the wind. Rachel was a rock. Hannah had to speak with her. She put on her terry cloth robe and ran to the door to welcome Rachel.

"Hello, Rachel dear!" Hannah's mood had just flipped 180 degrees. Rachel's eyes bugged wide as she looked at Hannah. In her rush to meet Rachel,

Hannah had neglected to tie the sash of her robe, which now fell open.

"Is Saturday your day for washing clothes, Hannah?"

Hannah looked down at the open robe and her naked body and gasped as she waved Rachel in, closed the door, and tried to knot the robe belt all at once. Hannah ran to her bedroom to find something to put on.

"I'm so sorry, Rachel," she screamed from her bedroom. "I forgot. I didn't notice. I was thinking. I wasn't thinking. You know..." Hannah was scarlet from shame but knew that somehow Rachel would understand.

Rachel nodded as she surveyed Hannah's apartment. She saw the knife on the floor and tea and water all over the kitchen table. She knew that something was up. Still, with Hannah, she needed to be careful about what she said.

"Sure, no problem. Happens to me all the time. I am forever seeing my friends naked. Even happens to me in wintertime."

Hannah came out of the bedroom in jeans and a T-shirt and greeted Rachel with a big hug. It was a tight "Hannah hug" that Rachel had grown very attached to. Unfortunately, it also meant that there was something troubling Hannah. Rachel thought it best to go slow.

"Heading to the park to play some tennis against the wall. Thought you might like to come and then maybe go to lunch? Didn't realize you were busy with pole dancing and knife-throwing practice," she said, motioning toward the floor. "Anything you want to talk about?"

Hannah looked directly into Rachel's soft blue eyes. Rachel liked to joke and be silly at times, but Hannah always felt that, at her core, Rachel cared. Hannah smiled at her good friend and then reached out to take her hands.

"It was such a bad night. Walter is such a jerk." She proceeded to tell Rachel about Walter, Reid, and the two women. As she listened to Hannah speak, Rachel thought about their friendship. Rachel realized that she and Hannah had a very odd relationship. On the one hand, Hannah would go into deep detail about some current event that was bothering her, telling Rachel things about herself that Rachel was not convinced she would share with Hannah were she in the same situation. On the other hand, Rachel knew almost nothing about Hannah's past beyond the time when their friendship began a few years ago. Hannah was both a very public and very private person with Rachel all at once. In this situation, without the background of Hannah's life experience, Rachel couldn't draw the equation between Hannah's intense sadness and Walter's evening of (barely) straying. Naked crying jags and knives in the linoleum seemed to be a bit of an overreaction, but she knew her friend was hurt, so she didn't want to minimize it.

Rachel wouldn't admit it, even to herself, but her own affection for Hannah was getting in the way of her being perfectly objective about a relationship of which she was slightly jealous. She smiled at Hannah to relax and console her.

"Men. Can't live with 'em, can't live with 'em." Hannah smiled back. She understood that Rachel didn't understand. She understood that Walter didn't understand. Yet, she also understood that she would never live a life of happiness, satisfaction, and honesty if she could never tell another how she lived. Hannah was trapped in a spider's web spun from violence, degradation, and self-loathing. How could she ever expect redemption if she refused to release the tapestries of her life that proved her worth?

Hannah decided to join Rachel in a game of wall tennis. She felt it oddly appropriate that they both enjoyed a game that could never be won.

• • •

Walter never called Hannah again after the Halloween party. He was embarrassed and ashamed of his behavior. He knew that Hannah needed him, yet he'd left her alone. Reid said that this only proved that Hannah was weak and beneath the high standard of quality that Walter should expect in his woman. Walter knew that this was silly talk, the bluster of a small and insignificant man. Walter knew it took more strength for Hannah to walk away than it would have taken her to stay with him.

Walter dated other women, of course, but his mind always wandered back to the look on Hannah's face, her two different-colored eyes, and the feeling of pure joy he felt when he held her and she spoke to his eyes.

He was also haunted by Hannah's statement about "only letting a bit of Hannah out" that night. He felt that for all the time he had spent with her, he only knew the small bit that she'd shown him.

There were times when he'd wonder why he ever let her go.

• • •

Rachel had developed a different view of Hannah over the year. She had spent time speaking with her and consoling her after the Great Naked Knife Incident (which is how Rachel referenced the memory in her friendly shorthand). Rachel spent many hours and used many different approaches to find out more about Hannah. There were so many places where Hannah would stop her. Rachel viewed Hannah as a fortress made impregnable and strong because she felt so weak emotionally all the time.

The more Rachel engaged with Hannah, the more she respected and loved her. To Rachel's mind, a person so obviously wracked with pain who still functioned as well as Hannah was worthy of her love and attention. Every time she prodded Hannah into divulging some small piece of her previously undisclosed existence, she felt the intimacy between them grow. This made Rachel quite happy.

One night, Rachel brought over a photo album filled with pictures of her childhood. She wanted Hannah to know all about her life before they'd met. Over a bottle of chilled white wine, Rachel told stories about her tree-climbing, berry-picking, jelly-making childhood. She told Hannah about her favorite Christmas present and birthday celebrations.

The more she drank, the more details she revealed. At times, Rachel's eyes became moist from laughter at some silly memory of her past or a ridiculous story about her uncles or aunts. She often placed her hand on Hannah's knee as she spoke to her. At times, she allowed her hand to gently stroke Hannah's thigh. Rachel wanted to draw Hannah into her life completely. With each glass of wine, she became more and more convinced that tonight could be the night.

What Rachel did not—and could not—know was that Hannah was barely maintaining her buoyancy in this deep and troubled sea of the past. She couldn't let Rachel know how awful she felt, how every word of Rachel's stories was just a bitter reminder of all the words that she could not say, all the stories she could not tell. She needed to laugh at all the right places in Rachel's narrative. She couldn't penalize Rachel for her wretched past.

For those who could see, Hannah had completely withdrawn from the discussion. A robotic android was functioning as her partner would like. A tear began to form at the corner of her eye after one of Rachel's more outrageous stories of the past.

Rachel, quite drunk by now, assumed that Hannah had teared up at the humor of the story which she had just told. Moving closer to Hannah, she put her arm around her shoulders and placed her hand on the middle of Hannah's thigh. She smiled and looked at Hannah.

"Unbelievable, isn't it? What a hoot!"

Hannah smiled, albeit nervously, because she had lost track of what Rachel was saying minutes ago. Recovering, she looked into Rachel's eyes and said, "Yes, very, very funny."

Rachel's attraction to Hannah had reached its zenith. The mixture of too much wine and too much fun had finally emboldened her to do what she had been wanting to do for months. Rachel moved closer to Hannah, embraced her, and began to kiss her on the lips.

Hannah allowed Rachel to kiss her and kissed her back. She had no idea how she could possibly stop her. As Rachel grew more amorous, Hannah became more uncomfortable. She didn't really know what to do. Finally, she summoned the courage to gently push Rachel away.

Rachel looked embarrassed and hurt.

"I'm sorry, Rachel. I just can't. I can't do it. Please don't ask me why, but I can't. I love you, but I can't." Hannah was stammering and upset. Hannah hated the thought of hurting her good friend, but she could not maintain any more charades in her life.

Rachel was mortified. The fever heat of attraction and wine was now converted to intense embarrassment. How could she have been so wrong about Hannah? She closed her book of memories, pushed the glass of wine away, and turned to look at Hannah one more time.

Rachel saw sadness in Hannah's eyes, but she also saw a cold, almost lifeless resignation that she had never noticed before. To Rachel, it seemed that Hannah's expression reflected a feeling that spoke to some repetitive pattern of despair. This moment was just another "thing" in Hannah's life. This "thing" was a small tragedy to Rachel.

Wordlessly, Rachel packed up her things and moved to leave Hannah's apartment. She knew that it was going to be quite some time before she ever returned, but she didn't think Hannah understood that. As they approached the door together in silence, Rachel tapped Hannah's hand slightly and smiled, valiantly.

"We'll get by this, OK? We'll talk it out. Another day, another time. OK?" Rachel held Hannah's hand gently as she prepared to leave.

Hannah, who had no idea at all of how she should deal with this situation, nodded at her friend's suggestion. She hugged her slightly. They said goodbye and Hannah locked the door behind her. Completely confused, Hannah walked past all the half-filled glasses and crumb-filled plates on her coffee table. She ended up in her bedroom, where she let herself fall face first onto her bed. Hannah grasped her pillow with her left hand and punched it with her right. Then she banged her head on her bed a few times and cried herself to sleep.

Hannah had not drawn the shade in her bedroom. The morning sun found the corner of her eyelid and propped it open in what was, to Hannah, an untimely moment. A mockingbird sat on her flower box, and its call, along with the bright morning sun, caused Hannah to slowly raise herself from her bed.

She had a tinny taste in her mouth that she wanted to erase immediately. Too much wine always left that taste behind, and Hannah never liked it much. She moved toward her bathroom to brush her teeth, wash her face, and gargle.

She considered herself in the bathroom mirror. Her skin was pale, and she could see the wrinkles that depressed her. Her hair was flat and disheveled. Her eyes seemed to be too distant for Hannah. She felt as though she was looking at herself looking at herself in the mirror, her emotional detachment reflected before her and reflected before it was reflected before her. She had tried to explain this feeling to Walter once, without great success.

What was she going to do now? She had no man in her life. Last night, she had alienated her best friend in the world. She knew that Rachel would never come back, although she doubted that Rachel realized that yet. Her life, which had always been without access to a living past, now had no prospects for the future.

She found it curious that, just then, Walter crept back into her mind. She recalled that horrible night at the party, his horrible friend, Reid. Still, Walter was a man she had thought she could trust on some level. Where was he now?

For a while, she used to look for him on busy city streets, in the crowded aisles of clothing stores or supermarkets. At times, she'd go to train stations or the bustling bars he enjoyed, hoping to get a glimpse of him again.

After a while, she gave up. She resigned herself to never seeing him again. Today was different. Somehow, the utter hopelessness of her situation had provided Hannah with an odd vision of hope. She began to get excited about the prospect of bumping into Walter one more time. Maybe they could rekindle what was the embryonic magic of a relationship newly formed. Maybe he'd be happy to see her again!

With hope in her heart, Hannah patrolled the crowded streets of the city in hope of finding the one person in the world who could provide her with redemption that day. Six hours later, hungry and tired, Hannah returned to her apartment feeling foolish and alone.

Hannah found something to eat. She prepared a cup of tea and tried to divine how a woman as smart as she could be so stupid. She didn't want to end her life hopeless and alone. Hannah was as sad as she had ever been in her life.

The greyish purple light of dusk had now become evening black. Hannah sat alone on the couch in her apartment, her feet up on her coffee table, a large cushion clutched before her. At times, she faded into a semi-sleeping state; at times, she just sat and stared at the blackness before her as the evening lights of the city behind her provided an uneven glow to her apartment.

Hannah woke to the light of a slate grey Sunday. There were no birds on her flower box, no sun upon her eyelids. Her lower back ached from an evening of sleeping upright. Her neck seemed locked into an unnatural position. She ran her hands through unkempt hair and struggled to extricate herself from the couch. She padded to the kitchen to make herself a cup of tea and some toast. She was as hungry as she had been in some time. She promised herself that she would do something constructive after breakfast—she would stay in this funk no longer. She was having a hard time believing in herself, but today was the day she was going to try. She approached her morning shower with a newfound determination.

Hannah decided a very hot shower would be best. She used the shower to relax her muscles and ease her pain. She washed herself slowly, noticing things about her body she had not noticed before. The freckles on her arms seemed to be fading into one large, faint discoloration. The birthmark upon her left thigh, which she always described as the fingerprint of God, was glowing in the steam of the shower. There were faint scars and awful marks that would never let her forget her past. She thought that her thighs were growing thick. Part of her new resolve should probably be applied to a workout regimen. She looked at a body framed by streams of shampoo bubbles. She felt that she was not as beautiful as she used to be. She was not as innocent as she was that day; she never would be again. Why had she been selected as the one who would be fouled forever?

Hannah thought that she heard her doorbell ringing but dismissed the idea because she had neither friends nor family to visit. She had just dried her hair, which was now scattered in all directions, when she heard it ring again. Hannah reached for her white terry cloth robe and hustled to her apartment door. As she approached, she saw two white sheets of paper lying facedown on the floor. First, she looked through her peephole. Seeing no one there and finding it odd, she reached for the papers on the ground before her. Flipping the papers over, she found them to be identical. As she read them, she heard children squealing in the courtyard below. The flyers showed a hand-drawn announcement of a "costumed event" to be held at the park down the street. All in her building were invited. There'd be a maypole dance, candy for the children, and an appearance by the Great Pumpkin. Fun to be had by all! It was scheduled to begin in a half hour's time and run throughout the afternoon.

Hannah slapped her head. Halloween! My God, it's Halloween and I have no candy for the children. As she thought this, her "Uncle Eddie" crossed to the corner of her mind. She pushed him away with the power of denial and determination over her years of suppression of things past.

Frantically, she ran about her apartment looking for coins so that she could offer some satisfaction to any trick-or-treaters who rang her bell.

She then paused to look at the flyers she held in her hands. Old Hannah would have tossed them away. She'd be fearful of people she did not know, costumed to conceal their true identities for their own fun and enjoyment. She'd be afraid that people would laugh at her, or ignore her, or, worse yet, want to know more about the woman beneath the costume.

Hannah wanted to change her life. She considered a costume. An artist? A French painter? These required little effort and would not likely move any guest to laughter or unhealthy curiosity. It was then that Hannah had a moment of clarity, a personal epiphany.

I must be Elizabeth, she thought. I will not go if I cannot find that costume and become Elizabeth. I must know that things that have been done can be undone.

She ran to her closet, dug deep in the back, and found the dress she had worn a year before. She ran to the bathroom to concoct the alabaster makeup she had concocted a year before. She put on her dress and applied the makeup carefully. She found the strings of pearls for her hair and carefully entwined the pearls with each braid that she used to encircle her face. She found her slate blue contacts and inserted them in her eyes. Fully in character, she paused to consider herself one last time.

She looked in the mirror and marveled at her transformation. She had become Elizabeth again. The dress fit perfectly. She was actually excited to be going to this event. She noticed she needed lipstick and applied a pale pink shade that complemented the grey eyes, pearl-strewn hair, and alabaster face perfectly. For a moment, she smiled at herself in the mirror. Even she thought that she looked pretty.

She picked up a flyer she had left on the couch and rushed to the park to join the party that would already be in progress.

As she approached the appointed spot, she saw nothing and grew concerned. There was no maypole. There were no children, or games, or candy. For a moment, she stood motionless in the park, looking in all directions for any signs of a party or costumes or people. She saw a few isolated heads of children dressed and going somewhere else. In anger and desperation, she let her hands fall by her side. Who would play such a cruel joke on her? Rachel? No, Rachel was embarrassed and hurt, but not mad. Who then?

As she considered these issues, her gaze was drawn to a small clearing surrounded by trees that seemed to be lit in an odd way by the sun, which was just breaking through the clouds. Seated at a picnic bench was a man with his back to the path, dressed in what appeared to be medieval clothing. He held his head in his hand and seemed to be staring off into space.

Another partygoer fooled by the notice? Hannah cautiously approached the man from behind. When she was about fifteen feet away, she called to him.

"Hello. Are you here for the Halloween event?" Hannah stood in the shadows of the trees while she spoke.

The man did not turn toward her. Instead, he held one of the flyers aloft in his left hand. "Did you get one of these?"

Hannah's eyes brightened at the prospect of not being the only fool living in the city.

"Yes, yes I did. Where is everybody? Are we early?"

The man in the odd clothing still refused to turn around. His voice was strange and his reply was odd. "No, I am afraid that we are about a year or so too late." The man finally turned to face Hannah as he spoke.

Let me not to the marriage of true minds
Admit impediments. Love is not love
Which alters when it alteration finds,
Or bends with the remover to remove:
O no! it is an ever-fixed mark
That looks on tempests and is never shaken;
It is the star to every wandering bark,
Whose worth's unknown, although his height be taken.
Love's not Time's fool, though rosy lips and cheeks
Within his bending sickle's compass come:
Love alters not with his brief hours and weeks,
But bears it out even to the edge of doom.
If this be error and upon me proved,
I never writ, nor no man ever loved.

Hannah was rooted beneath the trees. She didn't know what she should do. Should she run towards Walter or run away as fast as she could? Should she scream about the immediate joy or remember the pain? As he finished the sonnet, she decided to keep her distance and speak.

"That was just beautiful, Walter. You memorized the entire thing!" She was, in fact, touched by this on a most romantic level. She also noticed that Walter had developed crow's-feet at the corners of his eyes and the hair at his temples had the faintest hint of grey. Hannah saw everything she ever found attractive about Walter at that moment. Tears of joy began to form in her eyes.

"But how is it that you are here? Where is everyone else? How...?" Hannah was excited and completely confused.

"The invite says all are welcome." Walter smiled. "Only we two were actually invited. I didn't know how else to set up a date to see you again. I didn't have the courage to call." He stepped closer to her to see if he could read her reaction to his admission of guilt.

Hannah's jaw dropped and she spun a tight circle as she continued to search for other guests. Finally, fully cognizant of what Walter had manipulated, she walked slowly from beneath the trees and allowed her hands to hold Walter's.

Walter continued to smile as she approached. He thought that her costume accented every part of Hannah's body perfectly. As Hannah came near and Walter held her hands tightly, he stared at the face of the woman before him. The alabaster makeup could not cover the beauty that had attracted him before. Her eyes were steely blue, and they seemed to twinkle as she stared at him. Walter realized that the tears that were beginning to form in Hannah's eyes provided a certain refraction of the sunlight that fell upon the opening in the glade. Hannah's eyes darted slowly from one of Walter's eyes to the other as she tried to fully appreciate the man before her. She smiled at him, but Walter felt that there was a hint of sadness, a deep and permanent sadness that could not leave Hannah's face. She seemed so happy and so sad at exactly the same time.

Hannah's lips were pursed and thin. The light pink lip gloss highlighted her beautiful smile. The beauty mark on the left side of her nose had not disappeared, and as Walter stared at Hannah, he was happy to re-visit it again. Walter let one of Hannah's hands go as he stroked the side of her face and felt her smooth, soft skin.

Finally, he looked at the golden frame to Hannah's face—her hair. He loved the way her hair looked when she wore it as she did today—tightly braided and framing her face. He adored the way her hair looked when she let it fall straight to the middle of her back.

Hannah looked up at Walter and let her hands caress the nape of his neck.

"I've missed you so much," she said, as the tears continued to form in her eyes. "There is so much that I want to tell you. There is so much I can never tell you." Hannah had pushed herself away from Walter's embrace as she fixed her eyes upon Walter's.

Walter smiled at Hannah as he attempted to break the tone of extreme seriousness which she had adopted.

Hannah would have none of it. She shook Walter slightly and fixed her eyes upon him again.

"There is so much that I will never tell you, Walter. There is just so much. If you'd like, I will share every moment of our future; please do not ask me to share one moment of my past. What's done cannot be un-done." Here she averted her gaze as tears began to stream down her cheeks.

Walter lifted her chin and smiled at Hannah one more time. "No questions. I promise."

Hannah placed her finger at the corner of her eye to stop the crying. She smiled at Walter as rivulets were formed across the alabaster on her face.

She smiled sheepishly and sniffled slightly as she nuzzled into Walter's shoulder to be comforted and feel loved again.

Walter could not believe it. His plan was working better than he could have ever dreamed. Soon, he'd be making love with Hannah again. How great was that?

Of Cypress & Sunflowers

I guess I thought that it was going to be a good day. My father had kicked my mother down the stairs, and I had caught her on the landing. This helped to break her fall. I screamed an infantile insult. At the time, this was the most sincere form of hatred that I knew. Tears were in my eyes, but I could not let him see me cry. I was seven at the time and standing up to him as best I could. I couldn't let him see the misty-eyed weakness of a child hurt by the actions of an ir-rational man. He hurt me more than the breaking of my mother's fall did. He forced me to deny that a part of my day ever existed. He forced me to want to forget a part of my childhood.

"I went to my Little League game and played pretty well. I had a few hits, and I hadn't made any mistakes in the field. It was the last inning and the score was tied. I think the bases were loaded, though it may have been first and third. There were two outs. The ball was hit hard and bounced a bit to my right. I moved slightly and made a backhanded stab. As I pulled the ball out of my glove, the moment seemed suspended in time. I could see the stitches of the ball and the stamped insignia of our league on the cowhide.

"I can still see the moment in my mind's eye today. I saw my hand grip the stitches and throw the ball. I watched in dismay as the ball sailed over our first baseman's head. Our team lost and I was crushed. For the second time that day, it was all I could do to keep from crying. Everyone tried to make me feel better with words of inane consolation, words that seemed empty to me even then. I felt awful.

"I guess I could have lived with it. I mean, all the kids made errors at one time or another. It was especially hard because there was no one from my family there to pat me on the back or take me out to get a hamburger. I put my mitt in the basket on my bicycle. I watched all the other kids leave with their moms, or dads, or both, and I wondered what it was like to live like that.

"I especially hated to see Tom Gilroy's family at the game. They had a station wagon. Station wagons have always represented home to me. Station wagons were what real families used to drive around town. I resented station wagons because I knew we'd never get one. My father didn't think they were practical. My mother thought they were too expensive.

"I always stopped at the candy store on my way home. I used to buy bubblegum cigars. Green was my favorite, though at times I bought yellow or pink. I'd lean against the wall outside the candy store and pretend I was smoking. I guess that I was trying to waste as much time as I could before I went home.

"I'd get home and no one would be talking. My mom or dad might ask me who won and I'd tell them. They didn't ask much more. If I told my dad that I had made an error, he'd make an 'I told you so' type of harrumph.

"Sometimes my mom would cook us dinner on Saturday nights, but most of the time we would call for pizza. I knew what the Gilroys were having every Saturday night because they would discuss it at the game. They always seemed so happy. I never understood it.

"I remember one night when my father was hitting my mother so hard that she started to bleed. I was very young. I thought she was going to die. I screamed at my father and tried to push him away. He shoved me against the wall. My left arm was pinned beneath me. I had only my right arm to protect me. I could not protect myself. He hit me repeatedly and broke my arm. I screamed for God to stop him and finally he did.

"My mother's mouth bleeding and my arm broken, we went to the hospital and had our injuries repaired. I hated him so. I had no defense. I could only continue to forget incident after incident. I didn't know what else I could do."

The psychiatrist sat back in his chair looking carefully into the eyes of his patient, maintaining a completely nondescript expression. He picked up his twelve-cent pen and placed it between his teeth and into the corner of his mouth. "Tell me, why did you decide to become a painter?"

"I cannot write. I do not speak well. I cannot communicate with people. I could do nothing else. I have a talent. It is not between my ears. It is in my hands. I know this. I have seen it."

The artist's hands trembled slightly. He propped an elbow on his doctor's desk and rested his forehead between his thumb and forefinger. "Yet, I have not seen it manifested in my work. I paint in contour lines or like that silly man who paints the velvet pictures of tiger heads. My paintings are too exact, too perfect. There is no rot in my apples. There are no scratches on my furniture. All of my faces are without blemish. My art is not art. It is simply pictures. These pictures are not me. When I look at my hands, I see the power of creation waiting to be unleashed, but I cannot get at it. It is hidden by flesh and bone and blood. Sometimes, I just want to cut through my hands to get at it. I've never been able to harness this creative force."

"Yes. I see. But what ever made you become an artist?"

"There is something very wonderful about art. I can look at a mountain filled with trees without leaves and paint a summer scene. I can control the outcome. I can paint what is there or what is not. I can paint what I'd like to see rather than what I've been forced to see. I can leave all the pain and anguish behind. I can make people happy with my work."

"Have you?" asked the psychiatrist.

"Have I what?"

"Have you made people happy with your work?"

"Well…no. I have not considered my work good enough for public display. I don't need that kind of rejection right now."

"Let me venture to say that you are not qualified to judge your work now or at any time in the foreseeable future. You have no respect for yourself. You do not see the goodness that you possess. You don't know what talent you have." The psychiatrist looked at the Baby Ben clock on his desk.

Vincent's eyes misted. "Doctor…" His head turned slowly to the right as he tried to dab at the moisture that was suspended at the edge of his right eye. What he was about to say was very difficult. "Doctor…"

The psychiatrist tapped his Baby Ben slightly. It was as though he was tapping the last minute of Vincent's time out of the clock.

"Sorry, Vincent. Our time together for today has just run out."

Vincent opened his mouth to protest but realized that it was no use. The good doctor was always very stern about deadlines, and once his appointed time was up, Vincent was always unceremoniously dumped from his doctor's office into the world that existed outside.

Everything in Manhattan was releasing heat as Vincent walked away from the doctor's office. Busses were spewing tall, thin walls of heated carbon monoxide. The buildings were still trying to release heat stored in their bricks from a week of record-high temperatures. It was a steamy day in August from which there was never any natural relief. The sun was shrouded by clouds and made indistinct by the waves of humidity and smog which seemed to bounce off the pavement and up to the sky in a never-ending undulation of human sweat and city filth. Older businessmen mopped their brows and the napes of their necks with handkerchiefs soaked from a similar motion made moments before. Young men buttoned the middle button of their five hundred dollar suits and pretended to be cool. Women of all ages wore as little as possible, diverting the attention of most every man and causing public work and construction projects to be delayed all over the city.

Vincent was distracted by the buzz of the city and disturbed by the heat. He was looking for a place that was air conditioned and cheap. He wanted a few hours of relief before he went home to his fifth-floor walk-up that had one fan by his bed and a view of an alley.

He was wandering the village, window-shopping for things he could not afford, when he came upon a sign that would be his salvation that afternoon. A local artist with whom he was casually acquainted was having a show in what looked to be an air-conditioned gallery. He thought that a couple hours of seemingly intelligent nods and quasi-intellectual chatter with people who thought themselves truly gifted would be one way to cool off that afternoon.

He was also a little interested in this gentleman's work, so he did not feel entirely Machiavellian in his plan.

Vincent knew Olaf as a painter of great flamboyance who felt he touched the soul of the city and all of the people in it. Whether he was questioned about it or not, he could often be heard discussing his great powers of perception to any who would care enough to listen, or pretend to do so. He wore "normal" clothes, so he wasn't "outwardly flamboyant"; rather, he chose to prove his flamboyance of existence by participating in activities that were disparately common. He attended all the local sports bars, and attempted to discuss his female conquests with those who did not know him well. He attended all the avant-garde and trendy art shows, and read financial periodicals in public library reading rooms. To speak to Olaf, one would think that there was not a museum in the city he had not visited, nor a restaurant in which he had not eaten.

Vincent thought that Olaf was a man overwrought, a man "fishing in too many waterholes," trying too hard to be something to everybody. Vincent knew him well enough to know that all that Olaf did was contrived toward a purpose, but he could never quite get a handle on who Olaf truly wanted to be. He wondered why Olaf would maintain so many charades in his life. Was it ennui, or some deeper problem?

Still, when speaking with friends about Olaf, he was careful not to be too staunch in his defense. Vincent wanted to make it quite clear that he was not a fan of the man, and he did not want others to think he was anything more than intellectually sympathetic to Olaf. He felt that "intellectually sympathetic" meant nothing more than cowardly and hypocritical, but it was a posture he felt compelled to take. He was smiling to himself as he thought of all the different levels on which he did not trust Olaf, when he saw that Olaf was approaching him.

Olaf, mistaking Vincent's smirk for a smile of recognition, approached him as soon as he entered the gallery. As usual, Olaf was dressed "normally": His blue jeans, green T-shirt, and sneakers could have been worn by any man on the street. His paintings— and the show's attendees—gave a more profound picture of the man. Olaf smiled broadly as he approached and seemed to be genuinely happy that Vincent would drop by to see his work.

"So good to see you, Vincent. I must say I am a bit surprised, but pleasantly so. I thought you were a bit more structured in your approach to art. I did not realize that you also appreciated the Neoclassical Rococo Revival. How did you find out about my showing?"

Vincent was nothing if not an honest man. He had never heard about the Neoclassical Rococo Revival style, nor was he sure that it even existed. He suspected that Olaf, the man of great flamboyance, had developed this mythical style to help define himself to himself. He had not known about Olaf's showing until he almost bumped into the hand-painted sign on the street. But Vincent did want to enjoy Olaf's air conditioning for just a little while longer, so he answered very carefully.

"News of your show is out on the street, Olaf. I'm sure that you will find that many others will come in to view your work today. As for the NRR (you do call it that also, don't you?) style, I am interested in all forms of art and expression. How late are you open today?"

Olaf smiled again and ran his hands through his somewhat matted and greasy hair. "Open till 5 this afternoon and from 7 to 10 tonight. Isn't that great?"

Vincent nodded absentmindedly, "Yeah, great." He was actually computing the hours of air-conditioned time available to him divided by the amount of time he could put up with Olaf and his work. He would want to take a break to eat, of course.

Just then, an older woman with very pale legs and varicose veins walked by. Her feet were encased in plastic sandals. She wore a flowered cotton dress that had the unfortunate characteristic of revealing all this woman had to offer. She had a large ball of curly brown, severely knotted hair sitting atop her head. Vincent imagined her to be an aging poetess, a communist most likely, full of hatred and resentment for anything that was "standard" or "typically American." She probably liked most anything that could be remotely classified as "avant-garde" or "artsy."

She stopped in front of a white canvas with a thin green line running down its middle that Olaf called "TREE." Vincent wondered how Olaf justified his art to himself when he looked at his reflection in the mirror each morning.

"It is magnificent, isn't it?"

Vincent started at the voice behind him and turned to see Olaf smiling. "I'm sorry, could you repeat that?"

"It really sort of pulls you in, doesn't it?"

"What does?"

"You know," Olaf extended his hand to direct Vincent's attention. "Chris."

"Chris? I don't believe we've been introduced."

"Oh, don't be silly!" Olaf giggled. "I'll introduce you then. Come with me."

He led Vincent towards the room's centerpiece—a tall, brown phallic structure that resembled a melted tree. Vincent noticed a label on the floor at the base. It read "CHRIS."

"Well, here we are. Vincent, this is 'Chris.' 'Chris,' this is Vincent." Olaf beamed.

Vincent looked up at the melted tree before him and smiled weakly, at a loss for words.

"Yes, this is 'Chris,'" Olaf repeated proudly. "I think of all of my works as living beings, Vincent. 'Chris,' short for 'Christian,' reflects the disintegrating interest in Christian values and cultures."

As Olaf stood beside him describing 'Chris,' Vincent noticed a woman smiling at him from across the room. She held a leather folio close to her chest, and there was a cheap, white pen tucked behind her ear. Her eyebrows had been darkened artificially, and there were black streaks throughout her blonde hair. She wore deep red lipstick and a short black skirt.

Vincent mumbled something about Chris's artistic merit and then asked to be excused so that he could appreciate the rest of Olaf's oeuvre on his own.

For his part, Olaf was relieved to be rid of Vincent, who was becoming a bit of a bore. He had not responded to 'Chris' with the enthusiasm Olaf had expected from a fellow artist. Then again, one could hardly call Vincent's work "art." He stepped over to speak with the woman in plastic shoes who stood in front of "TREE."

Vincent began to walk around in the slow, appreciative gait that most save for galleries and museums. He looked carefully at each work of art. The canvasses were filled with bright colors and body parts.

He could not believe that anyone would buy an "Olaf Original" and marveled that Olaf was able to show these works at all. Still, Olaf had the opportunity to have a public showing, which was more than Vincent could claim. Olaf had been involved in the world of art since he was a child, while Vincent came to it much later. No one knew Vincent. Those who did know his work thought that it lacked an inventive approach. Vincent was beginning to bemoan his fate when he happened to see the blonde again.

She was taking notes before one of Olaf's massive works that occupied an entire wall. The hard, wide lines of primary colors seemed to be clashing and jockeying for the position most likely to catch the eye. Vincent found it to be mildly interesting, so he thought that he'd approach the painting and the blonde simultaneously. He felt that if he could get an idea about her opinion of Olaf's art, he'd have sufficient insight into the woman. As he approached, he attempted to look over her shoulder to read what she was writing.

Abruptly, she swung around and found herself nose to nose with Vincent. Startled, she let out a little gasp, which attracted the attention of the people around them. She looked annoyed.

"Are you accustomed to sneaking up on strangers?" Her tone was motherly, her face was agitated. Vincent thought that her blue eyes were beautiful.

"Ah…no…" was his intelligent reply.

The woman's face softened slightly. "Well, you are certainly an eloquent sort." Her voice descended to a whisper, "Be nice to me or I'll put you on a first name basis with another one of these god-awful pieces of art." Her smile was much broader now, and there was a certain twinkle in her eye that Vincent found to be irresistible. She extended her hand. "Vanessa White, Channel 47."

Vincent was nonplussed and struggled to speak mildly intelligible English. "I am Vincent. Vincent Van Hausen. I live nearby and I have no channel." Vanessa laughed and shook his hand. "Well good for you, Vincent. I'm damn glad to meet you. Wait a second. Aren't you in publishing? I think I've heard of you somewhere."

"Publishing? Me? No." Vincent was still struggling mightily with his native tongue.

"Oh my God, you're not in TV, are you? We're not rivals under the same flag, are we?"

Happy to feel himself regaining his composure, Vincent moved on to multisyllabic words. "I'm not in TV; actually, I'm an artist and housepainter. You are in TV, though? That's interesting."

"Well, mildly interesting I guess. Yes, I am in TV. I guess it's just a bad habit that I introduce myself that way. I am here today to see if there is anything in this show that might be worth ten or twelve seconds on our station's special on local unknown artists. So far, I've neither seen nor heard anything that I'd think would be worthwhile other than your delightful interplay with Olaf."

"Oh, you heard that, did you?" Vincent said sheepishly.

"Yes, I did. I'll tell you what, with your good looks and natural wit, you'd be great on TV. It's a shame that you don't have any talent."

"Well, I can paint. How do you know that I don't have any talent?"

"Our introductions were slightly different. I said I was from Channel 47, you said you paint houses and pictures. You don't have a show; Olaf (who has no talent) does; so if p = q, you have no talent. You are not a candidate for the little screen." Vanessa's eyes were playfully glassy and her tongue appeared just between her teeth as she fully enjoyed taunting this strange man.

Vincent's mind flashed back to the discussion with his psychiatrist earlier that day. He grew serious and defensive. "I know I have talent. Perhaps you are not a great judge of people."

Vanessa could see that she might have gone too far with this man. What if he were some sort of brooding, intense artist whom she might have turned off with her bluntness and humor? She backed away from playfulness and moved the conversation to more serious issues. "I was only kidding, Vincent. I'd like to see anything you've done. Maybe it'll make the special."

Vanessa wasn't quite sure why she had volunteered to look at Vincent's paintings. She didn't know him, and she didn't know what she would say or do if she really hated them. There wasn't much that was new and good.

Vincent wondered if he looked as uncomfortable as he felt. An invitation to have his paintings viewed by another was something that terrified him. That the viewer would be a member of the media was something that was inconceivable. He tried to come up with a way of saying no without offending this kind and beautiful woman. More importantly, he wanted to say no without sounding like an antisocial weirdo. He decided to try honesty.

"I must say that I call myself an artist though no painting has been purchased and no discerning eyes have evaluated my work." Vincent hated to speak about his "work"; it seemed so pretentious to him. "I create. I don't know if I create well," he continued. The uncomfortable nature of any discussion about his "work" caused Vincent's speech to seem halting; he was almost stammering as he tried to enunciate what he felt. "I don't know who has created well and if they knew they were creating well when they created. I am convinced that I sound like a fool. I am concerned that if you see my work, that you will be convinced that I am a fool. That would truly be a shame, because I think that otherwise we could get along quite well."

Vanessa looked at Vincent and saw sincerity and pain struggling to form a public display of honesty. He looked away from her as he spoke. Usually, she did not trust a person who would not look her in the eye when they spoke. Here, she suspected that this man was looking away from her because he was revealing some ultimate truth, some hidden key to his life that he was loath to give away. These words were gushing from some remote place in his being, and to stop them would be like trying to stop a flow of magma from some long dormant volcano. She knew that when he was finished, she would not know what to say. She thought that she might change the subject and tell a joke, but that might make him think that she was belittling his thought. She felt compelled to say something kind and soft without the hint of pity that she felt he would resent. But she could not help it, she pitied the man.

She decided to be upbeat, change the subject, and acknowledge his thought all at once, "I agree with you, Vincent. I think that we could get along quite well. But, I also have a job to do. What do you say we do this: First, I am duty bound to finish looking at Olaf's show, but I hope that you will accompany me. After that, I think we should have dinner together. Channel 47 will pay, I assure you. Finally, and only if you feel it's right, you can show me your works and, good or bad, we'll talk about them all you want. What do you think?"

Vincent was extremely pleased by the offer. It gave him time to get to know Vanessa better and enjoy her company, and it also gave him time to find a reason why she should not be allowed to see his works. Why did he ever tell her that he was an artist? He always found a way to do something stupid. "I'd love to have the opportunity to escort a nice lady like you around." Vincent smiled at Vanessa, and she smiled back as she hooked her arm in his.

They walked in slow circles around Olaf's work. Vincent was a bit uncomfortable because Vanessa didn't say much as she took notes and evaluated the art. At times, Vincent and Vanessa would stand beside each other and look at a piece. Vincent's head would tilt to the right, and he would be squinting. Vanessa would tilt to the left, and her eyes appeared closed. Both were trying to find the proper perspective, the correct view that would make Olaf's work more appealing.

When they caught one's another glance, they would smile or roll their eyes, attempting to wordlessly communicate, building an invisible bridge to unite them. At times, Vincent would strategically place himself far away from Vanessa so that he could appreciate the whole person—view this being as she existed in the world around her. Given distance of time and space, would she still seem as flawless to him as she did when they were close and he could appreciate and wonder at each perfect detail of her physical being?

Vincent thought that Vanessa was one of the prettiest women he had seen in quite some time. Her black skirt, which ended mid-thigh, highlighted her shapely legs. At times, she bent forward slightly and Vincent was captivated by her perfect figure accentuated by black, high-heeled shoes and a deep blue blouse that provided an ample view of her significant cleavage. If Vanessa noticed him staring, her eyes would brighten, her beautiful red lips would separate, and she'd smile broadly and wink at him. Vincent was smitten and Vanessa seemed agreeable.

Although Vanessa already had enough for Olaf's piece of her report, she lingered in the gallery, trying to assess Vincent and his intentions. Artists could be so weird and, at times, so imbalanced that Vanessa wanted to be sure that Vincent was "OK" before she actually went out to dinner with him. She thought that he was very cute, and when she caught him staring at her, she was pleasantly surprised by how childlike and awkward he was.

After a forty-five-minute Kabuki dance of pretending to evaluate art without merit and a man who might have some, Vanessa sidled up to Vincent and asked, "Ready for dinner?"

With a stern look of seriousness, Vincent stared directly into Vanessa's blue eyes and said, "Going to dinner with you sounds wonderful, but I'd really like to spend more quality time with 'Chris.'" He extended his hand to point to the melting phallic art. They both laughed.

"I'm sorry, Vincent, but this art is me." Vincent turned to find Olaf standing behind him. With tears in his eyes, Olaf said, "I'm sorry you feel the need to mock it in my presence."

Vincent's eyes met Vanessa's, and both of them shared a moment of embarrassment and shock. Vincent held up his hand as if the action could stop Olaf's tears. "Olaf…I'm sorry. It was a stupid joke. I'm sorry. I…we didn't mean anything by it. I am so, so sorry."

Olaf choked out his words through the tears. "There was no 'we,' Vincent. It was you! Now, I have to ask you to leave. Vanessa, you may stay to finish your report." A few tears followed distinct routes around Olaf's chubby cheeks and dripped off of his chin.

Vincent turned to Vanessa with a plaintive look in his eyes. He knew he had to leave, but he didn't want to leave without her—they were supposed to be having dinner! With a minor shrug of his shoulders, he made his way to the front door and departed. He shambled toward the street corner and decided to wait for Vanessa there.

Inside the gallery, Olaf begged Vanessa to understand his work. He put his hands on Vanessa's shoulders as he spoke. "I hope you won't let this two-bit speed artist influence your opinion of me and my art. My work is so relevant. My style…NRR…so few do it well. So few do it at all. It isn't easy."

Olaf was blubbering now and Vanessa just wanted to get away. She was concerned that this little breakdown might prevent her from dining with the "two-bit speed artist" (whatever that was) who was roaming the streets without her. Still, she had to repair the damage.

"It's OK, Olaf. I'm already done with my piece. What he says has no impact on how I feel about your work. You'll get some time in my report—don't worry." Vanessa gently touched Olaf's arm as she finished her comment to him. She wanted to console him without providing false hope.

Olaf wiped his eyes, nose, and cheeks as he tried to regain control of himself. Vanessa's comments made him feel better. He wiped his hand on his pants and then extended it to Vanessa in an act of reconciliation.

Vanessa tapped Olaf's elbow as she spoke. "It's OK. You'll get some time, don't worry. I'll be in touch—OK?"

Silently, Olaf shook his head "yes" and turned away. Vanessa made her way to the exit as quickly as she could.

A wave of city heat, a cacophony of city sounds, greeted Vanessa as she left the gallery. She needed to find Vincent. Her eyes darted toward different points on the city sidewalks. So many people—where could he be? She turned right; her eyes were filled with worry, anticipation, and excitement. Finally, she saw him, looking equally anxious. He waved and they walked toward each other.

As they got closer, a sense of relief bridged the distance between them. The awkward situation with Olaf created a bond that neither had anticipated. They moved together quickly now. They needed to find a quiet place where they could sit and talk. They passed a small Italian restaurant named John's. It was empty, so they decided to go in. As they sat down and relaxed, they smiled at each other, simultaneously realizing that their criteria for a restaurant choice was counterintuitive and logically flawed.

Vanessa suggested they order a bottle of wine. Once the wine was uncorked and poured and they each had their first sip, a sense of calm seemed to settle between them.

Vanessa held her wine glass in a very considered manner, peered over the rim, and stared into Vincent's eyes in a way that Vincent found both disarming and sexy.

Slowly, Vanessa took another sip of wine as she considered Vincent. "What the devil is a 'speed artist' anyway?"

Vincent returned Vanessa's stare as he considered his answer. It was then that he noticed how long Vanessa's fingers were. They were not adorned with any jewelry. Her fingers were wrapped about the circumference of the glass as she spoke. While she waited for Vincent's reply, she slowly licked her lips and then sipped some more wine.

Vanessa suspected that Vincent was uncomfortable with her question. His eyes began to dart from side to side. His hesitation seemed to speak to his level of unease. She noticed the brilliant blue of his eyes. There seemed to be a translucent shade over them as he considered her question. Sexy eyes, Vanessa thought. The more she considered Vincent's appearance, the more attractive he looked to her. She smiled at Vincent to help him to feel more at ease.

Vincent was always somewhat ashamed of what he did for a living. He averted his eyes before he spoke. He was afraid that Vanessa might think less of him if she knew. Finally, he decided that he had to speak. "A speed artist can do this." He pulled a pencil out of his pocket, took a paper napkin, and drew an elephant's head in no time.

Vanessa watched in amazement as Vincent crafted cityscapes and mountain scenes on napkin after napkin in no time. "That's awesome," she said, with genuine surprise. "How long have you been doing this type of stuff?"

Vincent was somewhat put back by Vanessa's overly enthusiastic reaction. "I've been able to do this as long as I could draw." He smiled an awkward smile.

Vanessa found his reaction charming. "What else can you draw?"

Vincent stared at Vanessa for a few seconds before he decided to answer. He wondered how far into his personal vault he should allow this female to come on their first time out together. Throwing caution to the wind, he looked her in the eye in a very serious way and then he spoke again. "I can have you draw five lines in any way you want on a piece of paper. I can have you tell me what you would have me draw. Within three minutes, I will incorporate all lines and draw the picture of your choice."

With her mental meter tilting toward "drunk," Vanessa said a little too loudly, "No way! No one can do that!" She called to the waiter and asked that he bring some paper for them to use.

Vanessa drew five completely unrelated lines on the page. She passed the paper and pencil to Vincent as she removed her watch from her wrist. Vanessa took a large gulp of her wine, looked at Vincent, and then looked at her watch. "Draw me…an elephant."

Vincent turned the page around a few times and stuck the pencil in his mouth as he considered Vanessa's unrelated lines and request. Suddenly, he took the pencil out of his mouth and began to draw. Vanessa thought that she heard Vincent talk to himself as he drew. Within two minutes, a perfectly formed elephant was before her.

Vanessa was nonplussed. "A giraffe…a monkey… an East Side condominium." The more she challenged Vincent, the better he seemed to be. The wine flowed easily. The laughs were frequent. At the end of the night, she was happy to take Vincent home and to her bed.

They began to date regularly. Vincent was still reluctant to show Vanessa his work. It took three months before Vanessa was allowed into Vincent's apartment. It took Vanessa another month before she could fully share her opinion with Vincent.

His pictures were like photos, lovely photos—drawings of empty benches, drawings of playgrounds without children. Vanessa felt Vincent's pain while she appreciated his talent. Vanessa felt that Channel 47 needed an artist like Vincent and told him so.

"We're trying to get viewers involved in the creation and appreciation of art. What would you think of a show where you spend the majority of the time on the construction of an artistic piece (how to draw a mountain in the distance, how to paint a tall pine tree) followed by a fun segment where you take your talent for speed drawing and construct a picture suggested by an audience member from the five lines they provide?"

Vincent's employment prospects were pretty thin. He was also developing a deepening love for Vanessa. If he had a good job, he could ask her to marry him. The job did involve art, after all. What more could he ask for?

Vincent wrapped his arms around Vanessa and kissed her on the cheek. Holding her tightly, he whispered in her ear. "If you can sell it to your network, I'll do it in a nanosecond."

Vanessa pulled her body away from his for a second so that she could look into his eyes. She smiled broadly as she looked at Vincent. She felt that this was going to be the start of something wonderful. "I can sell anything to my network. You are going to be great…"

The show was called "The Artist's Corner," and it debuted six months later. Because Vincent had the habit of speaking to himself as he drew, he became known as the mumbling artist. People who wanted to learn about art and how to paint were regular viewers. The "Fun with Five Lines" segment was a huge hit, especially with kids who enthusiastically sent challenging five-line puzzles that Vincent would make into art. When he failed to "beat the challenge," the child contestant would receive a paint set and small certificate acknowledging that he/she had beaten "The Artist's Corner."

Assorted ne'er-do-wells watched the show to listen to Vincent's running commentary about painting that sometimes ventured into the truly bizarre. His unconscious signature phrase—"This beauty of a tree, here"—became a drinking cure for college kids around the country. In short, his show was a huge success.

It was a beautiful spring day in Manhattan. The air was cool. The trees were budding. A softly massaging zephyr was moving air about the town; a high blue sky gave hope for more of the same tomorrow. Vincent was heading home after the show, walking to his East Village apartment. As he approached a playground on his left, he heard several loud blasts and saw plumes of smoke and large flames. Odd music was blaring in the background. A tall, masked man in the center of the conflagration was singing unintelligible songs and gesticulating wildly.

It was a nice day for a brief tour of hell, so Vincent thought that he would explore the situation. The man who was singing and doing a manic dance removed his mask and pointed at Vincent as he approached. Vincent wasn't quite sure, but he felt like he was being accused of something by this stranger who, upon closer examination, had tattoos running down both of his arms.

A guttural groan was coming out of the loudspeakers. "Evil, evil, evil..." The word was being endlessly repeated and seemed to be describing Vincent.

It was then that Vincent recognized the wild man. It was Olaf! Vincent smiled and waved to Olaf as Olaf accused him of being an evildoer, the anti-Christ. Vincent stood outside the circle that Olaf had spray-painted on the ground. He guessed that Olaf had either lost his mind entirely or that he was into some different kind of Neoclassical Rococo Revival Performance Art style. In either case, old guilt dies hard. Vincent wanted to have a conversation with Olaf.

Olaf spent another few minutes screaming obscenities and blaming Vincent for untold crimes and uncommitted sins. Soon, the fires died out, the smoke subsided, and the raucous music stopped. Olaf mopped his brow with a red rag he had taken from his back pocket and approached Vincent.

Vincent was amazed at how Olaf had aged. His face was rutted with deep furrows, his eyes were sunken, and the area around them was puffy. He was bald, but, for some reason, this did not surprise Vincent at all.

Olaf shut off his microphone as he got closer to Vincent. "Hello, Vincent," he said, his voice sounding softer and less guttural than it had just moments before. "How is the world of TV realism and speed drawing for kids?" Olaf meant this to be an insult, though Vincent did not take it that way.

"Actually, things are good. I don't mind the TV show; I actually sort of like it. The money is good, and Vanessa and I are very happy. We may even get married soon." Vincent surprised himself with his final comment. While he thought of Vanessa constantly and wanted to be married, he had never admitted it publicly. Why tell Olaf, of all people? Vincent wondered about himself sometimes.

"Married?" Wide-eyed and mocking, Olaf's voice went up a few octaves. "An artiste like you marrying that woman who does not understand the first thing about art?" Olaf's comments were dripping with sarcasm, but a guilty Vincent refused to take the bait.

Vincent smiled at Olaf. "Yes, Olaf, married. Can you imagine? I am, no, we are very happy, and we have you to thank. If it hadn't been for your show, we never would have met. I never would have been on TV. We have you to thank for it all." Vincent extended his hand, but Olaf would not shake it.

"I will not hear this," he said. "The community is ashamed of you, Vincent. You make a mockery of fine artists everywhere. Artists should not be speed drawing crabs and turtles on television. They should be suffering through life, learning the pain, feeling the angst, creating beauty from traditionally unhappy experiences. Artists do not talk to themselves about some 'beauty of a tree' when the tree is too real to be beautiful." Olaf had faded into a faux Serbian accent as he spoke. Vincent was beginning to fear that he had been drawn into another performance art tableau.

Vincent looked into Olaf's eyes once more. "I am happy, Olaf. My art, my love has taken me there. If my art is not good enough for you or this 'community' of which you speak, so be it. I am what I am, not what I can pretend to be."

Olaf drew himself up and seemed somewhat outraged. Vincent had touched a sensitive spot in his existence "You think me a pretender?" The faux Serb artist had returned. "You know nothing. You do not feel. You do not love. You do not suffer. You are a monkey. You dance to the tune of the public's organ grinder and people throw shekels at your feet."

Vincent had had enough of Olaf's insults. It was a day too nice to be spending with such a bitter man. He extended his hand to say goodbye to Olaf, and

Olaf spat at him. Vincent looked at his hand and then he looked at Olaf. "I'm sorry I upset you. I've got to go. Good luck with your performance art and the Neoclassical Rococo Revival or whatever you call it." Vincent couldn't help but chuckle slightly as he walked away.

Olaf was incensed and screamed at Vincent as he walked away. "I am an artist. You are nothing. I have my work. You have a simple-minded woman who knows nothing about art and idiot children who idolize you. You are nothing. Nothing!" Olaf screamed his closing remarks as loudly as he could. Vincent just waved at Olaf and smiled to himself as he walked away. He was now convinced that Olaf had, indeed, lost his mind.

When he got home, he told Vanessa all about his meeting with Olaf. Her eyes twinkled when he mentioned marriage. She was thrilled that Vincent was thinking that way. She was more thrilled that Vincent didn't notice that she noticed.

That night, Olaf went to the clubs to drink. He had been removed from the playground after some parents complained about his act being inappropriate for children to see. The police gave him a summons and sent him on his way.

Olaf blamed Vincent. If he had not stopped to speak with him, the others would have seen the perfection of his performance and the police would have never been called. Olaf was not only jealous of Vincent's success, but he hated that Vincent was happy. Olaf's life had taken too many turns off the road to happiness. Olaf had spent too much time at oxbows of thought.

Olaf spent that night like an angry hobo: drinking, drugging, and sleeping on subway grates. His anger was complete; he was the artist—poor and unappreciated—and a speed artist like Vincent was living the good life. There was no justice in the world.

The next morning, Vanessa and Vincent woke in each other's arms. Vincent's right arm held her close. Vanessa felt secure and happy. They dressed and headed to work as they always did. They had decided that they would go to their favorite restaurant after the show. Vanessa thought that something special might happen at the restaurant, so she wore Vincent's favorite outfit—the same one she had worn the day they first met.

Vincent smiled when he saw her dressed, and told her that, to him, she was simply the most beautiful woman in all the world. They left the apartment with her arm tightly entwined with his. As they walked down the street, they joked about things they saw or people they encountered on the road to the studio.

After one night of vagrancy, Olaf decided that this could be his newest form of performance art. He had no money, so he would beg. The reactions he got from people when he begged would be his "street art" available for all to see. The reactions of the people watching the reactions of the people would make the art more timeless and universal. Each layer of observation would be more distant than the core transaction, yet each would relate to that action. "Like an A-bomb," he thought. "Reactions radiating art from ground zero." He fingered the stiletto he'd bought for protection as he worked on his plan.

Unfortunately for Olaf, the stench of old booze and body odor, along with his unkempt appearance, had most people avoiding him, thinking "vagrant" rather than "street artist." His pleas for money became more belligerent, the reactions more extreme. He decided to use the element of surprise for his next piece. A handsome couple was walking his way—he would try to scare them into giving him money.

As Vincent and Vanessa approached, Olaf jumped out before them and pushed them against a wall. For a moment, they were pinned there, Vincent's left arm wedged into Vanessa's side.

Olaf brandished his stiletto. "Give me some money."

Vanessa screamed and Vincent tried to push him away with his right hand. His efforts were ineffectual. At that moment, he realized that he had used the same hand to throw the ball away so many years ago when everyone had depended upon him. He tried to push at Olaf again, and Olaf waved his stiletto through the air, slicing Vincent's right hand open. There was no art, no power to create in that hand—only blood and muscle, which was beginning to leak all over the couple and the sidewalk. Olaf licked the blood from the knife for artistic effect and looked at the woman screaming. He saw her legs, he saw "that dress," "that blouse"—this was the woman who had ruined his art. She would become artwork now. He sliced both legs, he sliced her face. She crumpled to the ground. Blood was everywhere. Vincent fell with her. He was screaming because of his own pain. He was screaming at the sight of the woman he loved, dying on the street. He tried to defend himself with his useless right hand, but he couldn't do it.

The thrill of creation was pumping Olaf's being. He sliced the throat of the screaming man to silence him. It did. He plunged the stiletto into the heart of the dying woman.

Blood was everywhere. Olaf heard police sirens getting louder. He looked at the crumpled couple before him, a pile of dead flesh and instantly rotting tissue. For a moment, he smiled to himself.

"Pure art won today. The hacks are dead on the street." As the police approached him cautiously with guns drawn, they told him to drop the weapon.

Olaf paused for a moment and hurled the stiletto into Vincent's left hand, which had now become exposed. Blood began to ooze out of his lifeless hand. Just as had been true with his right hand, neither "artistic talent" nor "creative force" flowed from the wound, only the remaining drops of his life's blood that had been lurking beneath the surface.

The King

The King was in rare form tonight. After spending the better part of two hours in Casey's Gin Mill eating peanuts and drinking Golden Tequila, he had decided it was time to engage the fundamental Christian tourists who had just arrived from North Carolina that day.

The tourists were kindhearted and lost. They had been wandering the city for over two hours looking for the Chrysler Building, and they had made the mistake of sharing their table with The King shortly after he had consumed his sixth tumbler of "Gold." He instantly made them adopted drinking buddies for the day and began to regale them with odd stories and humorous anecdotes culled from his very wild life. Murray, Frank, and Doug viewed their interaction with The King as part of their tourist experience. There was no one like The King in North Carolina; the unique nature of his personality made him a tourist attraction who would be spoken about back home like the other sights they had seen. Remembered far more completely than their visit to the Museum of Modern Art, The King was a man unlike any they had encountered before.

The King's pale face was the picture of inebriation. His eyes were brown and seemingly without pupils—like a doll's eyes. The top two buttons of his Sea Green on Hunter Green plaid shirt were open, and one collar formed a forty-five-degree angle across his chest. His hair stood straight up at different locations on his scalp because The King had a habit of pulling his hair at odd angles when he told a story which he felt was particularly entertaining. The sleeves of his shirt were cuffed at the elbow, and he often gesticulated wildly when he spoke.

Feeling comfortable with his newfound friends and knowing that they were Christian fundamentalists, he decided to bring out some religious material to see if he could generate some interesting responses.

He tapped the table for attention. "Frankie, Murray, Doug...you guys remember the birth of Jesus?"

Wondering where this was going, they all smiled politely (the way people do in North Carolina) and nodded in the affirmative.

"Remember the manger, the animals, the straw...?"
Again they nodded and smiled.

"Do you remember the THREE KINGS?" He raised his voice on the last two words for emphasis.

Again the men nodded and, unconsciously, Murray murmured, "Of course." The King felt he had planted the hook deep down his companions' throats and smiled as he delivered the punch line for this sequence of questioning. "Where did the three kings go?"

For a moment, the combination of too much alcohol and a general lack of understanding of the point The King was trying to make caused the men to sit dumbfounded and blinking slowly as they searched for a proper, polite response. Finally, Murray asked, "What are you talking about, King?" His friends muttered in support and affirmation.

The King smiled and repeated his question for dramatic effect. "Where did the Three Kings go?"

The men were puzzled, but at least more animate in their response this time. Almost in chorus, they said, "To see the baby Jesus, of course! Everyone knows that!" They looked at each other with reassuring smiles.

The King nodded and smiled at each man individually and the group collectively. "No, no…you guys don't get it. I want to know where the kings went *after* they saw the baby Jesus."

Murray, Frank, and Doug looked at each other and then at The King. Then they looked at each other again with great question in their eyes. Finally, it was Murray who broke the silence of the group. "Honestly, King, I'm not quite sure. They had to avoid Herod at all costs. I imagine they just returned to their king-doms...their homeland."

Murray looked at the wooden table before him and spread a ringlet of water around on its surface as he considered the answer that he had just given The King. It struck him strangely. He couldn't believe he'd ever have to say that he was unsure about anything in the Bible. He thought that he had the Bible pretty much committed to memory. He said it again, more thoughtfully and meditatively, "I'm not quite sure, King. I know they needed to avoid Herod."

The King smiled the self-satisfied smile of sweet victory. This was a game he could play every day. He loved the moment. He loved the blank looks on the faces of these strangers that he had adopted as friends. The King looked at Murray and smiled more softly and with a slight air of understanding. "Don't worry about it, Murray. Don't worry about it. Your memory is not failing, your knowledge of the Bible is not flawed. No one knows what happened to the three kings. It is as if they visited Jesus and turned to vapor. They are never mentioned in the Bible again. Trick question boys, trick question."

Murray, Frank, and Doug looked at each other to see if any among them could confirm or deny what The King had just said. They all wanted to reread the gospels immediately, but there was neither the time nor the opportunity.

The King re-engaged his audience. "Isn't that amazing? A star leads these guys to the savior of all mankind, and they don't become disciples or acolytes or prophets—they simply disappear from God's book. Wiped clean from God's thought or part of a more earthly metaphor?"

Mary was upset because she had to go to the bathroom. She had been sitting beside Francine listening to The King (it wasn't hard—The King always spoke too loudly) while sipping a sloe gin fizz. She had found the whole scene very entertaining and was loath to depart while The King was in mid-sentence, but Nature called. She would catch up with Francine when she returned.

Mary had often seen The King at Casey's and found him to be smart and very entertaining—but she also felt that his was a personality type that had a hard time noticing her in a crowd. He always seemed bigger than life to her, or at least he was a man with a personality bigger than the bar. There was a certain confident freedom in him that she admired, maybe because she found that lacking in her psyche. Mary could never command the attention of strangers; she admired those who did. Mary was shy and circumspect in almost everything she did. She never wanted to be a bother to anyone. The King was so different, but she admired his liveliness and thought his personality winsome and cute.

Francine wished that Mary had not gone to the bathroom. She would have never come out if Mary had not invited her. Francine did not like crowded places or alcohol. She was painfully shy and constantly fearful of all that surrounded her, no matter where she was. She had been listening to The King with Mary, but now that Mary was gone, her eyes darted about; she paid close attention to everything that invaded her line of sight as she sat in the bar. As The King spoke, she swore that she saw a mouse run past the legs of the table at which she was sitting. Francine was petrified and began to perspire.

One of Mary's friends once described Francine as the human embodiment of a neurotic squirrel. Francine was very slightly built, her chin almost non-existent. She looked athletic but not pretty. Her hair was shaved and styled in a way that made it look very much like the fur between the ears of a brown city squirrel. When she wanted to dress up and be stylish, she wore a leather Fossil bracelet with a primary color pattern broken by brown leather knots on some arbitrary basis. While Mary was gone, Francine wore her horn-rimmed glasses to be certain that she did not miss anything in life that could threaten her existence. She had begun to tap the table nervously when Mary finally returned.

Mary slid into her seat with an air of excitement and smiled at Francine as she sat down. "Well?"

Though relieved that Mary had returned, Francine was not ready for such an open-ended question and was startled by Mary's remark that certainly seemed to anticipate something. Francine touched the corner of her glasses, sat up efficiently in her chair, and regarded Mary with some trepidation as she said, "Well… what?"

Mary, exasperated by her friend, slammed the table with one hand and motioned toward The King and the tourists as she said, "The King…. What did he mean by 'a more earthly metaphor'? What did he say? What did they say?" Again, Mary motioned toward the group.

Francine was now completely confused. She looked into Mary's eyes as she spoke. "What on earth are you speaking about?"

Mary tried to explain to her timid and confused friend. "We were listening to The King speak about the Bible before I went to the bathroom. He was in mid-sentence on a point about the three kings before I left. I was waiting to hear what he had to say. I was hoping that you could tell me."

Finally Francine understood. "Oh, him…" (If she could have harrumphed, she would have.) "No, I wasn't listening to him. I find him rather vulgar. Plus, I believe that a mouse ran by while you were gone. I was rather concerned with that."

Mary was crestfallen. She had really wanted to know what he had to say. She turned to listen to the conversation at the next table, but it was hushed, punctuated by the guttural laughter one releases when he hears a particularly dirty joke. Mary assumed that The King's conversation with the strangers had degenerated to that.

For a moment, Mary let herself stare at The King as he spoke. Whenever she looked at him and then reviewed her thoughts later, she realized that, for her, The King was greater than the sum of his parts. He was good-looking, but not great. Physically fit, but not athletic. Witty, but not particularly funny, and smart without being impressively intelligent. Why was she so attracted to him? It couldn't really be because he filled in her gaps, her self-perceived weaknesses, could it? She thought he was the type of man that she could like if she knew him, but every time he spoke with her, she thought that something was lacking and she could never get the feel of exactly what it was. If there was time tonight, Mary was going to approach him again. At the very least, she wanted to find out the earthly metaphor of his Bible story.

The King was enjoying his time with the tourists. Their enthusiasm for all of his jokes, rants, and random thoughts motivated him to rant further. Those who had little use for The King described him as a black hole that sucked all the energy that fed him into a self-sustaining void serving nothing or no one. Others spoke of him as a planetary destroyer that cruised through the universe consuming all and discharging what was useless to him. His best friends called him self-centered and egotistical.

What none of them realized was that none of this talk had any effect on The King. The King needed to be The King or else he would die. He didn't have much use for any who would adore him. Those with whom he interacted did not know it, but they were characters in a play that The King created every day. Each day, the plot was different, but the ending was always the same—The King made sure that he was satisfied. Happiness did not matter—a satisfactory conclusion was the key. The King interacted with people to keep the play new and fresh, not to establish continuity or security. He never needed those things.

The three men from North Carolina all had trouble standing as they pushed themselves back from the table. One had finally realized that it was time to go, and the others were too drunk to disagree. They stumbled into each other slowly as each made their way to shake The King's hand and engage in one drunken embrace of acknowledgement and farewell. They had been taken to a place that they never expected to be by a young man they did not know, and while they might not have found enlightenment, they brought vague memories of good times to the door of the bar as they departed. Those memories would mostly disappear by morning—too much alcohol, too few touch points in reality that the men could share. They would never see The King again.

As for The King, he felt energized by his interaction with the three men from the South. He felt that each had brought something special to the evening for him. He had had many drinks, but neither his mind nor his spirit had been dulled; he felt fresher than he had when he awoke that day.

The King's other "accomplice" for the evening—he rarely called them "friends"—was also very inebriated. He had one more drink with The King, slapped the table, and announced that it was time to go. Feeling too good to end the evening right then, The King escorted his companion to the curb, poured him into a cab, and returned to the bar. The King was feeling great. The King was deeply ensconced in the beat of the moment. He had found the space between the tick and the tock. He wanted to celebrate, he didn't want to let it go.

Francine was beside herself with anxiety. Mice, men from North Carolina, The King, the crowds…it was all too much for her to bear any longer. She knew Mary didn't want to leave, but if she didn't get home soon, Francine felt her psyche was going to shatter like so many shards of glass.

With quiet terror in her eyes, she pulled on Mary's grey sweater to get her attention. Mary had been watching the front door of the bar as The King returned from the street. She felt an odd sense of relief when she saw The King walk back into the bar.

Sweat formed on the space between Francine's upper lip and nose as she feverishly tapped Mary's arm to get her attention. Finally, Mary turned to Francine. "What is it?" Her tone was agitated.

Francine's dark eyes darted from one side of the bar to the other as she spoke. "I've got to get out of here, Mary. Now. I'm sorry, but I can't take this place anymore. It's just too much for me."

Often, the overarching anxiety of her friend was a source of great consternation to Mary. Francine's weakness was off-putting and, at times, inconvenient. Tonight, Mary welcomed the opportunity to put Francine in a cab and send her home. She was actually rather happy to see her go. Mary had other plans for the evening.

"OK, dear…" She patted Francine's arm in an act of consolation and support. "How about I walk you outside and we'll get you a cab? I think I am going to stay here a while longer."

"Stay here???" Francine was shocked. "But the mice, the drunks, the people…"

Mary smiled reassuringly and spoke in a conde-scending yet conciliatory tone. "I'll be fine. Don't worry about me, dear. Let's go get you a ride home."

Francine nodded and wiped the hint of a tear away from the corner of her eye. She was happy to be going home. She was sad that her friend would not be going with her. Mary brought her outside, hailed her a cab, opened the back door, and hugged her ten-derly before Francine got in. Mary smiled sweetly and said, "See you soon," as she closed the door for her friend.

Francine waved meekly to Mary as the cab pulled away from the curb. Francine spread her legs wide, let her arms flop onto the seat, and allowed herself an audible sigh as the cab took her back to the safe house she called home.

Mary waved at Francine's cab as it pulled away. For one moment, she hesitated. She thought of hailing a cab for herself. Instead, she stood erect on the street, established a resolute attitude, and pushed the door of the bar so hard that it slammed against the wall as she entered. She'd never tried anything like this before, but she felt that tonight the night would be hers.

Though Francine might think otherwise, the crowd at the bar had thinned significantly, and it was rather easy for Mary to approach and order another sloe gin fizz. The bartender smiled at her as he delivered her drink, but she had absolutely no interest in him. She had returned to that bar to accomplish one goal; her only problem was that she had no clue, no plan on how to accomplish it.

It took Mary a few sips of sloe gin to summon up the courage to approach The King. When she looked up from her drink, she saw that he was watching her. His hair was still pulled rather wildly in every direction, his eyes were now slits in his face, and he weaved slightly as he leaned against the bar. As Mary approached, he rubbed the side of his face with his left hand and audibly took a breath of bar air.

"Was a time I smelt the odor of night-old cigarettes and the dim lights of a honky tonk. Now all I smell is filtered mediocrity and homogenous conformity." The King was speaking to no one and everyone again.

Mary was nervous as she spoke, and she didn't know exactly why she was about to do what she would do. She held out her hand and smiled. "My name is Mary. I couldn't help but hear you speaking before. I think you are quite funny and interesting and I wanted to say hello." The smile remained plastered on Mary's face, but inside she was devastated. Could her greeting be any more stilted, her approach any more sophomoric? She prayed that he could somehow see past all that and still engage in a conversation.

The King's eye slits narrowed even further as he considered the woman before him. He shook her hand and mumbled an incoherent greeting. A day of alcohol and entertainment was getting the better of him, and he needed a bed. He wasn't ready for a conversation with a human being, even though this one was quite pretty.

After shaking Mary's hand, he gave a little wave. "Too drunk, too drunk, speak another time." The King was falling fast. He grabbed at a cocktail napkin, scribbled his phone number upon it, and placed it in Mary's hand. "Call me."

The King pushed himself away from the bar, shoved the door open, and fell into a cab, which would take him home.

For a moment, Mary stood blinking, wondering what had just happened. He seemed fine before she approached him, and then he could barely walk or talk as he bolted through the door. She uncrumpled the napkin he had placed in her hand. In a script that was barely recognizable, he had scribbled "The King" with his phone number. For a moment, Mary wondered if this guy ever shared his true name with anyone. She became extremely uncomfortable as she felt that she was standing in the middle of the bar alone. She folded the napkin, put it in the pocket of her jeans, and went home.

Mary woke early the next day to go to church. She wore her favorite blue dress. As she walked to church, she mused about the goings-on from the night before. Mary was confused and yet hopeful. The fact that she had the courage to approach The King was a great step forward for her. If and how this relationship would ever play out was all she thought about during the service.

Back home, she went to her bedroom and took the folded napkin out of her pants pocket. She unfolded and placed it on her kitchen table, a passive reminder of the challenge she had set for herself.

It took a few days, but Mary finally picked the napkin up off the kitchen table and called The King. It took her a while to explain who she was and how she came to have his number. He told her that he met so many people that he had a hard time remembering faces and names. They arranged to meet for lunch. Mary felt that lunch would be a good time to catch The King, a time before he had embraced the world filled with strangers.

They met at a Greek restaurant that Mary knew well and was not very far from where she worked. The restaurant was famous for its fish. She was able to reserve a quiet table in the back of the restaurant, which she felt would be conducive to conversation. She also thought that the fish on the menu would slow The King's apparent penchant for drinking. Mary never knew of anyone who got very drunk when they ate fish.

Mary arrived first and watched the front door anxiously until he arrived. She waved to him as he came in, and (thankfully) he seemed to remember her as he returned a small wave in her general direction.

Mary was struck by how well kempt his hair was. He was also dressed casually but nattily she thought. Maybe this luncheon had some meaning to him also. He kissed her cheek as he said hello and sat down. Without hesitation he placed his napkin on his lap. The pair exchanged pleasantries and Mary was so uneasy about what she was going to say, she asked him the same question about his employment situation twice. He responded kindly and patiently to her questions and asked a lot about her past and the things she liked to do for fun.

Finally, Mary found a way to ask him about the story he was telling the tourists, and she asked him to fill her in about the part that she had missed. She was excited to know what he had said.

Mary was disheartened by the fact that The King could not remember the "more earthly metaphor" he had used in his description of the Magi. He told her that it happened to him all the time: On any given night, he routinely constructed wild theories and analogies that he tended to forget right after he said them because they were nothing more than moments within moments—earthly treasures that he dispensed to all who would listen. He rarely retained any of these for himself or committed them to memory.

The King and Mary began to date. She found his personality endlessly refreshing and interesting. He made her laugh. He made her think. Mary became a "regular" to The King's bar scene. After a time, she fell in love with him, and they spent many wonderful nights together. The only thing that bothered Mary was that The King would never attend church with her. He didn't believe, and he would not "simply accommodate" her wishes.

Mary grew more comfortable with The King's friends and faceless acquaintances. She was accepted by them but always felt a certain distance, a gap she could not bridge that prevented total acceptance. She found this to be troubling. Try as she might, she could not really penetrate the inner circles of The King's life.

It was a beautiful day in April when Mary's doctor confirmed what she was beginning to feel. Mary would deliver a "little King" (or would that be a Prince?), and his legacy would be carried through future generations. She could not wait to tell The King.

Mary arranged a romantic dinner at their apartment. She cooked his favorite dish. Three candles were set upon the table to symbolize the new family unit that she had created with The King. The dinner was prepared and ready to serve. Mary was bursting with excitement. She lit the candles on the table and sat at the seat facing the door to their apartment with her hands folded beneath and supporting her chin.

The King often referred to the front door as the "Portal to the New World" because they never knew what adventure lay beyond it each day.

Through the door, Mary heard The King fumbling with his keys and the lock and thought nothing of it. For Mary, the excitement of the moment they were about to share and her overarching anticipation of the great joy a baby could bring to their relationship consumed the atmosphere of their apartment as she waited for the door to open.

Suddenly, the front door flew open and The King came stumbling through. He bumped into a wall and almost knocked over the telephone stand as he raced toward the bathroom. As the addition of a small amount of air can destroy a vacuum, so did The King's blast from the vortex of his world destroy Mary's planned moment. The King mumbled words of apology as he left the bathroom and struggled to find their bed before he fell facedown upon it. He said something about a tough day at the job and meddling tourists who bought him too many drinks. For one moment, he seemed to see the sadness in Mary's eyes. He touched her cheek and said, "I love you, baby," as he passed out on the bed.

Mary was crying as she lifted his legs, undid his shoes, and put his legs upon the bed. For one moment, she wondered aloud how The King could do this to her and their baby. After a few minutes of crying and attempting to control herself, Mary found the strength to clear the table, throw out the food, and blow out the candles. She sat on the couch with her legs tucked beneath her and admonished herself for being angry or disappointed with The King. He didn't know anything about the "beyond special" dinner (which was all she told him) she had planned. He couldn't help himself when he felt like "stomping on the terra" in the course of everyday life. What she loved most about him would, at times, be the most maddening part of his personality. She needed to be stronger to overcome the many needs she knew The King had. At times, she felt that he didn't realize he had these needs himself.

The next day, after The King had fully recovered from the night before, Mary sat him down and shared the great news. Mary didn't know if it was a tinge of resentment that she felt about the evening before that made her think that The King did not receive the news of her pregnancy with appropriate excitement, or if her sense was actually true. It seemed to Mary that it took him a moment or two to say the right things and express proper joy at the prospect of the arrival of his child. Eventually, they hugged and kissed and Mary felt better about it all.

Mary was determined to be the perfect mom and the perfect pregnant mom. She read every book, evaluated every diet, and ate only foodstuff that would contribute to a healthy baby. She often asked The King to prepare the way for their child. She felt that they would need a larger flat, and the baby's room needed to be decorated. The King always found a way to postpone doing whatever she asked. He still ran with his beer buddies. He still spoke of the Portal to the New World. Mary sat home because she would not drink. Mary went to church because it was the right thing to do. Mary viewed the process of pregnancy as a righteous duty for any who were fortunate enough to become pregnant.

Though she had compromised some of her beliefs in this relationship with The King, she always felt that their love was an eternal love that would bring pleasure to the church. They would be married. Their baby would be baptized. All good things would be done in good time. Mary always felt comfort in her religion. Someday, The King would too. Together their love would be greater than the sum of the separate love they shared. Mary thought of these things always and believed them with all of her heart.

Mary still walked to church every Sunday. Her bright blue dress had grown tight as the baby inside her grew. As time went by, she wore a greyish purple dress that was appropriate for her growing body while being suitable for her church. For those who could notice, her hair had become matted and unkempt, her eyes watery and vacant—almost like the eyes of a doll. The pregnancy was becoming a burden, and as the term ended, she had trouble walking. At times, she found it hard to breathe.

Mary shuffled now when she walked to church. She became exhausted very easily. She was worried about the baby. She was worried about the pregnancy.

One Friday afternoon, she became so anxious that she decided to go to church to pray, hoping it would ease her mind. She left a note for The King. As she walked, each step became more difficult than the last. She was feeling pressure and pain. She opened the church doors and sat in a pew facing the crucifix, praying.

A solitary soprano was in the choir loft practicing, her back to the altar and the crucifix. The soprano was preparing for Sunday service. As Mary arrived, she heard the soprano announce to no one that she was to sing Psalm 103. Mary approached a convenient pew, but the voice of the soprano had consumed the church. Mary could barely hear herself pray, so she decided to approach the altar.

The soprano's singing sounded more and more like a dramatic reading filling the church with the words of the Psalm:

"As for man, his days are like grass; he flourishes like a flower of the field; for the wind passes over it, and it is gone, and its place knows it no more…"

As she walked, Mary's water broke. Her baby was about to be born, and she struggled to lay upon the altar. The soprano was still singing as Mary screamed in agony.

The soprano finished the psalm and turned to face the altar and leave the loft. She shrieked in horror at the scene before her and ran down the stairs of the loft and toward the altar. Mary lay in a pool of blood, her baby dead beside her. Hearing screams, the pastor of the parish ran from his office to the altar. As he approached, he assessed what had happened and did what he could to revive Mary and the baby, but without success.

The King approached the church door and heard a scream inside. He had read Mary's note and bought some things at the store before coming to the church. He went inside the church to find the pastor covered with blood, his head in his hands. The soprano was crying hysterically and repeatedly pleading for "God's mercy on these poor souls."

The King knew that there was nothing he could do. He placed the plastic bag with the three things he had bought on the pew before him. He genuflected slightly and left the church.

He was never seen, or heard from, again.

Life Comes to Spring

"Three hours is a long time to speak to anyone." Dave paused as he thought. "I mean, there is always dead air, uncomfortable silences, a perceptible energy drain on the conversation as time goes on. I mean, what are you supposed to say? What are you supposed to do?" Dave looked at his therapist, who was scratching notes on a yellow legal pad. "What do you do, Bob?"

Of course, Bob had only been half-listening to Dave's idle chatter. It had been some time since Bob found anything Dave said interesting. Besides, Bob was mentally preparing himself for his next patient, a twenty-something nymphomaniac who was considered the uglier of two sisters (at least, according to her). If this was the ugly one, Bob often wondered, what in the world did the sister look like?

"Well, revitalize the conversation. Lead it down an alternate path. When one is truly interested in someone else, anything the other person says can be a reason to expand or extend the conversation. I've done it many times." This was, of course, false, but Bob was trying to make a point with Dave.

"Go on. You've spoken to one person for three hours straight many times? Get out of here. That can't be true."

Bob tapped the clock before him. "And, unfortunately, we are out of time. We'll pick up this conversation just where we left it today. See you in two weeks."

Dave grumbled as he approached the door. He was feeling like a child again. Bob often made him feel that way. He could see the leering face of "Jimmy the Gyp." "Jimmy the Gyp" was Dave's neighborhood ice cream man when he was a child. Thinking all children stupid, he would often shortchange them. If they caught him, he would tell the children they were wrong and pull random change out of his pocket to prove his point; hence, his well-earned nickname. Dave was a smart kid. He knew Jimmy would often gyp him. Dave would complain loudly, but Jimmy would offer only a dismissive wave as a reply. That wave trumped all kids' complaints. Jimmy the Gyp could get behind the wheel of his pure white ice cream truck secure in the knowledge that he had stolen an extra ten cents from some little kids. The kids had learned that the adults held all the cards in their world. Being right didn't matter. Justice didn't matter. Jimmy could gyp because he was older than they. Jimmy would gyp because he could gyp. It was a painful lesson for a kid to learn.

Dave felt the same way about Bob now. "Bobby the Gyp" was stealing his money, and he wasn't even getting a stinking stale ice cream in return. Dave slung his coat over his shoulders and flung the hood up onto his head as he stalked away from the apartment with all the gargoyles on the wall, Bobby's place. No enemies internal, all beasties external, satisfaction guaranteed. Dave was angry. He didn't feel like he was getting any better. At times, he felt quite a bit worse.

• • •

Sheila loved to read. She would sit bolt upright while her mind consumed the words on the page with a voracious intensity unmatched by any other activity that she ever undertook. She had high-set cheekbones and large doe eyes that darted across the page as she read. She had a very trim figure and could comfortably wear tight clothes without regret. The only problem existed with her hands. They were too big. When she grasped a softcover book, her hands seemed to totally conceal its cover. Still, she would sit up straight and read, her right thumb and fingers supporting the spine of the book and her large left hand engulfing the rest of the book, leaving room for a fatty thumb to hold all previously read pages in place.

Sheila wished that she could find a way to find herself attractive. She longed for a day when she could fall in love with her physical appearance. People always told her that if she believed in herself, others would believe in her. Logically, would it not follow that if she found herself attractive, someone else would also find her appealing? The circular nature of the argument often led to her abandoning the concept of temporal, physical beauty. She found beauty in the rather solitary world of books and withdrew to that private world quite often. Her "bookishness" did not endear her to the world of which she desperately wanted to be a part; men were intimidated by her brains and the quality of her insights.

Sheila liked knowing that she was smart. There were times on Saturday nights, though, when she'd lay naked atop her bed, back upright, reading books before her dresser mirror. At times, she would take a break from reading and try to find the beauty in her body, the dormant sexuality in her breasts and face. There was a feeling of overarching freedom in her ability to read naked, yet there was never great joy in it. There was always a nagging something that tugged at her, pulling her down to the level state of depression to which she had grown accustomed. Sheila never looked quite right to Sheila. Her hands were too big; her face was too fat; there was something wrong with her hair. It didn't matter that others might feel the same thing about themselves; for Sheila, it was worse. At times, she was inconsolable. Otherwise, she was just miserable. She could not remember the last time she was truly happy. She could not remember an uncontrollable giggle or a twinkle-eyed wink at the absurd reality of a situation. She looked at others laughing and wondered how they did it. She wondered what it was like to be truly convivial. She hated the thought. She hated the reality that drove the thought. She looked in the mirror, and she couldn't help noticing the little brown mole that had been there since childhood. Her lips were pursed, and she noticed that they were cracking around the edges and that crow's-feet were forming at the corner of her eyes. Time was stomping across her face, and she was powerless to stop it.

• • •

Francis hated his name. He had hated it since he was a little kid. It never seemed to fit him. It was a name that sat on his shoulders perched on wrong bones that always made him shudder and shake as he tried to make it fit his body. For a time, he called himself Frankie, but that didn't work either. He wasn't a Frankie and he knew it. He tried Frank, but the endless comparisons to Sinatra grew tedious. Sinatra was a bully and a bulldog who happened to be able to sing, while Francis thought of himself as kind, sensitive, and concerned about others.

After a time, he gave up on Frankie and Frank and moved on to Fran, a name he felt was better suited to his personality. Of course, during the time it took for him to come up with a name that fit, he suffered what he perceived to be terrible trauma and ignominy as Frankie and Frank. Children teased him; girls spurned his sophomoric and awkward advances.

He had few friends in high school, and those who enjoyed his company often found him to be different and strange.

There was one episode during high school that ended up informing his image of self-loathing as he grew older, pervading his brain like a virus without an antidote. It was a party at Steve's house. The boys were in the kitchen drinking quarts of Colt 45 malt liquor. There were a few girls there also (which made this party special), and the boys were trying to get them to drink as much as possible so that there would be hope of adolescent love for later that night.

Steve was in mid-sentence as Francis/Frankie/Frank walked into the kitchen. "I mean, we all know that Frank is a loser. Let's face it. I mean, no one really takes him seriously, right? He's just too weird…" Steve's voice trailed off as he realized that Frank was in the room.

Frank pretended that he did not hear what Steve had said. He opened the refrigerator, pulled out a bottle of Colt 45, and headed for the patio. One of the girls in the room caught the sadness in his eyes. She knew Frank had heard Steve's words. Frank knew she knew. He could see her look of pity as he brushed by her on his way out.

Frank stood on the deck, drinking and looking up at the stars. An uneasy silence settled in the kitchen, and the kids scattered to other rooms in the house. It was as if they believed that, by not acknowledging it, and moving on to other venues, the moment of pain which they had just inflicted on Frank would dissipate along with their presence at the scene of the crime. None of them went to the patio to speak with Frank. Even the girl who had felt such sympathy for him did not know what to say. She went to the living room with her friends, where the conversation would be easier.

Outside, Frank choked down the cold beer. He did not want anyone to see the tears well up in his eyes. He did not want anyone to know how much he had been hurt or how desperately alone he felt. He was a high school senior who now knew for sure that he had no friends. Things would have to change.

He finished his beer without realizing that the kitchen was now empty behind him. He wanted to go home, but he didn't know how to get by the crowd in the kitchen without giving some indication of the hurt he felt. Finally, he decided to boldly walk through the mob and express his regrets about having to leave early. Since that was often the case with Frank (everyone knew what a shrew his mother could be), it was an excuse that the rest of the group could accept easily.

He turned and saw the empty kitchen, and a new wave of melancholy came over him. They really didn't care. Even Mary, who had seen his pain, had left with the others. Usually, women identified with Frank, appreciated his sensitive nature, and wanted to speak with him. At this low moment, he could not even rely on his usually reliable female friends to bail him out.

Frank hurried through the kitchen and towards the front door to make a quick exit. As he passed the living room, he waved to the group and said, "Mother calls. You know how she is. See you Monday."

Everyone waved and said goodbye, more than a bit relieved that Frank was leaving.

Frank was anxious to go, but he was not anxious to get home. He walked the quiet streets of his little town, which were empty save for the odd dog walkers who were creatures of the night by some natural necessity. They did not say hello to him and he did not say hello to them. Frank was perfectly happy in his transient anonymity.

Large oak trees lined the streets. Every 200 yards or so, Frank would pass by a streetlight and its blue laser glow would alter his appearance, the color of his hands and clothing. To Frank, there was something so sadly solitary about a streetlight. Frank could find sadness in anything and everything.

After a few glances at the heavens and a few ruminations on the surface of the moon, Frank approached the walk that led to the front door of his house. Mother resided on the other side. Frank blew into his hands one more time to be certain that there were no residual alcohol fumes she could smell on his breath. He sucked hard on a mint to get its final flavor bits to coat the lining of his mouth.

The porch light was on. The shrubs and bushes that lined the front of Frank's house shifted slightly in the breeze. Frank looked at the pewter doorknob. A feeling of foreboding washed over him—he was going to have to face her again. Lately, it seemed as if each day was worse than the one before. He grasped the doorknob and walked through the portal to his mother's reality. A perfect yellow light washed over the foyer. Each item was perfectly matched to the other, and none were out of place.

"Francis...Francis, is that you? Come in here, please."

Frank shuddered slightly as he walked into the front room to greet his mother. She was sitting in her favorite reading chair, a light perfectly centered upon the face of her book. She was wearing a black, tight-fitting dress which ended mid-thigh, black stockings, and those hideously pointed high heels that he hated so much.

Mother was always "dressed" until she went to bed, and then she wore elegant robes and nightgowns that never left her bedroom suite because "that was where they belonged." Her straight black hair cut a line across her forehead and beneath her chin as it halted just slightly above her shoulders. She wore ruby red lipstick all the time, and her eyebrows were jet black and often arched. Her eyes were always ablaze in their attention to whatever was going on around her. Frank noticed that she wasn't wearing a bra again.

His mother held out her perfectly manicured hand to greet Frank. She did not rise from her chair. The ruby red nail polish matched her lips perfectly. Frank wondered, for a moment, if he was supposed to kiss her hand—he grasped it thinly and sat down on the small couch across from her reading chair. Her left hand lay upon the open book before her. For a moment she diverted her attention from the book to focus on her son.

"Have you been drinking, Francis?" She focused her glare on his face.

"No, mom. Not at all." Could I look any guiltier, Francis thought, as he settled into the couch.

"Good, very good boy." Mom was self-satisfied again. Her Francis would not do anything wrong. Her Francis would not embarrass her.

She reached for her bookmark too quickly, causing it to flutter off the perfect white doily on the end table and land at her feet.

As she leaned over to pick it up, the low-cut front of her dress fell open and Francis found himself looking at much more of his mother than any lad should see. At that moment, she looked up at him from the floor. Anger flared as she grabbed the bookmark and waved it at him.

"You disgusting little man," she shouted. "Low-class, just like your father. I kicked him out of this house when you were a baby for lesser offenses than that. Get out of my sight. Up to your room." Francis' mom thrust the bookmark into her book, fixed her hair, and returned to her reading, seething.

Francis slowly shuffled out of the front room and up to his bedroom.

• • •

Dave walked the streets of the city for a while trying to shake his feelings of anger towards Bob. He often found solace in big cities and large crowds—he loved to lose himself in the people. After an hour or so, his anger dissipated and he decided to search for his friends at their favorite bar. His feet began to follow some familiar footpaths. His heart and spirit brightened as he approached Gabe's Bar.

Gabe's was owned by a beautiful Irish redhead named Sally McBride. When she named the bar, Sally had it in her head that she'd be far more likely to be robbed if she named it Sally's Place. Also, if she named it Sally's Place, she reckoned that any manner of clientele could frequent the spot (can you use another word—there seems to be too much "place"). She wanted a bar where real men would sit around and talk about "real issues," like wives and sports, stupid jokes and hookers, mistresses and exotic dancers— things she thought guys thought important.

Sally had a sense of people and of life not usually associated with a "woman's mind-set"—she liked guys who thought and spoke about things most women found "oafish." To Sally, these were the real people who powered civilization. These were the people who stomped on the Terra. These were the people who knew how to live.

Another problem with naming it Sally's Place was that every horny drunk would want to know who Sally was and how they could meet her. She wanted no part of that. Sally had some standards when she decided who it was that she would meet at Gabe's Bar. These might be the "salt of the earth" and "the movers of civilization," but, as Sally often said, "you definitely didn't want to date or, God forbid, marry one of them!"

Dave tried to see who was inside by peeking through the stained glass window before he entered. Sally was behind the bar and there were a few "Tourists"—the nickname regular customers gave to the non-regulars who would show up at Gabe's every once in a while. None of Dave's other friends were present, which disappointed him some, but he was able to pull up his favorite seat at the bar, and he always liked to speak with Sally.

"Brenda, what's up tonight?" This was another rule of Gabe's Bar required by Sally for all of her regulars. If there were any Tourists in the bar, and Sally was tending, they were to call her "Brenda." Sally had this thing about her privacy.

"Dave, my boy, things are just great. I feel like a million bucks, and I'm looking forward to tending some bar tonight." Her smile was easy and sincere. Her bright blue eyes glistened as she spoke. The small strand of pearls she wore around her neck accented her classic beauty perfectly. "How's about you? What news?" Sally poured Dave's favorite glass of beer and put it in front of him.

"Well, I've got a new job. I had been looking real hard for real long, and I finally got this gig which I enjoy. I transport monkeys between testing labs all over town."

"Monkeys?" Sally was trying to look serious. The Tourists started giggling in their seats.

"Yeah, monkeys… Why?" Dave felt a bit defensive about what he was saying without quite realizing how it would sound to someone who was actually listening for a change.

Sally smiled condescendingly. "I guess somebody's got to do it. How do you transport them, anyway? Aren't they heavy? Don't they smell?" A few of the Tourists made snorting noises as they attempted to contain their laughter.

Dave looked around the bar for a moment, concerned that others might be laughing at him. "Well, yeah, you put up to a dozen capuchins in a box with holes in the side, put the box on a dolly, and wheel them around town. They can make a racket, those little guys, and you've got to wear really thick gloves in case they bite."

"How did you get this job? Was there an ad in the paper?" Sally was biting the inside of her cheek and looking at Dave with a wide-eyed incredulity. This was not a job that one heard about every day!

A Tourist slapped the bar, convulsing with laughter. Dave looked around self-consciously and realized that the others were looking at him and smirking. He remembered a sad childhood, an ice cream man who gypped him, and all the girls who laughed in his face when he asked them out. He was upset and embarrassed, and he didn't want to say any more. He had been looking forward to having some time alone to speak with Sally. He liked his job. It may have been different, but he thought it was fun. He thought that Sally would be happy for him. Instead, she and the Tourists were laughing at him, as if he were some kind of joke.

The feeling was all too familiar. He hated the feeling. He hated the situation. He hated the fact that beads of "embarrassment sweat" were forming on his forehead as he sat in uncomfortable silence.

He tossed a five-dollar bill on the bar. "See you later, Sally." Dave stood up as tall as he could and walked toward the front door. He had a plan.

Sally looked down at the rubberized grate on the floor as Dave let the bar door slam behind him. Why couldn't she have played along and shown interest in what he was doing? Sure, it was weird, but she could have been nicer to him. He was always so nice to her. She sighed a deep sigh of resignation and sadness and turned to the Tourists with anger in her heart.

"Come on, all of you. Drink up. It's closing time."

"What are you talking about? It's eight o'clock!" said the Tourist who seemed to have had the most fun at Dave's expense.

Sally squinted one eye tightly and stared straight at the man's face. "It's closing time for you and your buddies. Now drink up and leave."

The Tourists looked quizzically at each other, shrugged their shoulders, finished their drinks, and left.

• • •

Sheila glanced at the clock on her bedside table. It was getting late, but it seemed pointless to go to sleep. That feeling of pointlessness struck Sheila more and more frequently lately. Sometimes, it was pointless to eat, or sleep, or read. At other times, it seemed that the concept of getting dressed when there was no one for whom she could get dressed seemed the most pointless activity of all. Then she would just lay there reading until she fell asleep and wake up cold or looking at her imperfect body that no one seemed particularly interested in.

Tonight was a bit different, though. Sheila looked at a photo on her bedside table. It was a picture of her taken at the falls. She was facing the sun, which reflected a pale orange, and squinting slightly. She had the most perfect smile on her face: She was perfectly placed in a perfect spot unconsciously enjoying a perfect moment.

A small smile was permitted to crease her face as she looked at this favorite picture of herself and reconnected with a happy moment in her past.

She put the picture down and glanced around her perfectly decorated room. The colors were all coordinated, the *objets d'art* were elegant and classic, and the room was orderly and well-kempt. Sheila smiled again. Then, her gaze wandered to the mirror. She saw flab in places it was not supposed to be, parts that were sagging, and a face that was creased and cragged. As Sheila's self-satisfied view of the world came crashing back to earth, her telephone rang.

"Sheila? It's me, Ed. From work," a voice said breathlessly. "Sorry to call so late, but I just got in from my trip to the coast. I was wondering if you might be free tomorrow night. Maybe dinner and a movie? I realize it's last minute, but I was hoping you'd be free."

Sheila was nonplussed. Ed was handsome and witty and young! Younger than she, and very successful. Why in the world would he be asking her out? Sheila was so deeply ensconced in her rumination that she almost neglected to answer his question.

"Tomorrow? Tomorrow would be great. Would you like me to come to your place?"

"No, I'll pick you up. You live over by the park, right?"

"Yes. Fourteen Delaware. How about dinner at eight and you can surprise me with the movie?" Sheila was buoyant and almost coquettish in her response.

"Fourteen Delaware—that's the most beautiful part of this town. What a great area to live in. Maybe we could do dinner at Tony's—is that good for you?"

"Great. Sounds wonderful."

"I can't wait to see you, Sheila. Tomorrow at eight, then?"

"Perfect. See you then." The unconscious smile had broadened into a wide grin of excitement on Sheila's face as she hung up the phone.

Ed Strauss. Wow. This could be great. A devilish glint of excitement and anticipation flashed across her face as she flopped down on her bed. What will I wear?

She sat up and looked into the mirror again, only to be reminded that Sheila was still there. Sheila the flabby, Sheila the old, Sheila who didn't look like her picture anymore. She picked the photo up and tossed it across the room in disgust.

I do live in a beautiful part of town. But it is Old, Fat Sheila's part of town. What does one do when they live in a beautiful place that they can't stand? How can someone ever grow to hate beauty? Sheila felt like she hated beauty at that moment. She hated her beautiful room in the beautiful part of town, with the picture of a beautiful, young, trim Sheila in it. What would Ed ever do if he saw the difference between young, trim Sheila and the fat old hag that she had become? This will be one and done, Sheila thought. What could she do to prevent it?

She paced her apartment. In every room, there was yet another picture of young and pretty Shelia— at graduation, with Mom, with Dad, with Mom and Dad, with brothers, with sisters, with family, with cousins, alone, with friends, smiling, serious. Through pictures, her apartment had become an altar to pretty Sheila. She went to the kitchen to get a pair of scissors. Sheila had a plan.

. . .

Francis sat on the edge of his bed and looked at the full moon framed by the window. The night being "moon bright" allowed him to see the pools and kids' toys that littered his neighbors' yards and the perfectly manicured bushes of his own. It was rock music versus classical played out in suburban green, Francis thought. Mother would probably say it was "upclass" versus "those people." She always tried to maintain a perfect appearance in her universe. She would not tolerate imperfection in her world. Imperfection was hateful and lazy, just like her ex-husband.

Francis looked at the moon and thought about what a miserable night it had been. Dissed by all of his friends and caught looking down his mother's dress— does it get much worse than that? He fell back onto his bed in frustration and disgust. What the hell was he going to do? How was he going to apologize to his mother without making matters worse?

The sedative power of the beer overtook him as he lay on his bed replaying the confrontation with his mother, and he fell asleep under the full moon. He woke about an hour and a half later, unaware that he had been asleep for so long. Feeling somewhat refreshed and less drunk, he got out of bed, took one more look at the moon, and decided to go downstairs to make it right with his mother.

He opened his door and looked down into the darkened front room. Assuming that his mom was still annoyed and had gone to her room to read, Francis knocked softly on her door. He thought he heard her say something, so he walked in to apologize.

Francis' mom always slept with a nightlight on. The soft light of a four-watt bulb made the shadows less harsh. Francis looked at his mother lying fast asleep on her pink Egyptian cotton sheets, wearing a short pink nightgown and nothing else. Francis thought she looked absolutely beautiful as she lay there. It was not her body that captivated his attention—though she still had the shape of a woman ten years younger.

Francis was taken by the beautifully elegant nightgown and the way it harmonized with the bed and the room to soften his mother's harsh edges. He wanted to touch the softness of the nightgown, but he knew it would wake her. Francis wondered what she thought of while she slept. Her peacefulness belied her endlessly agitated waking state.

He turned to the closet that held all of his mother's nightgowns. He let his fingers feel their silky texture, appreciate their subtle beauty. His eyes drifted to her makeup table and all the accoutrements his mother used to make herself perfect for the world. He let his fingers run atop the mascara brushes and nail polish.

Perfect for the world, he thought, what a concept!

Francis reached into the back of his mother's closet for a dress she never used, a nightgown he never saw. He folded them over his arm silently and stealthily escaped from his mother's room. He could go to the drugstore tomorrow for other things. Francis had a plan.

• • •

The streets of the city were dark and wet. The night seemed to have fallen harder tonight. The alleys were darker, the clouds seemed lower, and their pressure was palpable to Dave as he walked home alone. He looked at the faces of the people he passed as he walked. The strangers seemed to pause slightly as they glanced at him and then looked away. Dave was convinced that they felt he was strange and somehow unworthy of a full-faced encounter. He was becoming tired of the city. For the first time, he felt that it might be time to move. The only footfalls he heard on the street were his own. The noises of the city— sirens, horns, engines, and laughter—seemed distant sounds to him as he walked. He didn't feel like he was a part of anything; he didn't feel that he was capable of sharing the way he used to. He could laugh. He could have fun. But he was not having fun now.

Sadly, it was not his sense of detachment that was really bothering him—it was his inability to engage in anything that was meaningful to him. Everything seemed trivial.

Dave approached the door to his apartment and sighed as he pushed it open. Since he was a month-to-month renter, his landlord had chosen the apartment's décor and Dave had not done much to change it. Black-framed pictures of fresh fruit were evenly spaced on his chocolate brown living room walls. The dining area held a small Formica table surrounded by four high-backed, red-cushioned chairs. His bedroom was a study in almond and off-white. Even his bed frame and the drawers that held his clothes were bleached drab white. When he turned on the overhead light, he was consumed by the phosphorescent blandness of it all. Dave had never noticed that before tonight.

He had to get to bed early. He had a load of monkeys he had to move across town tomorrow. Though he'd only be working a half day, he wanted to be rested and ready.

He awoke to a beautiful day in the city. It was seventy degrees and sunny, a day so perfect that it helped to drive away some of yesterday's feelings of melancholy. He showered and dressed quickly. He had to pick up the monkeys by eight.

The move today was to be different than other moves Dave had made. He was taking a box of ten capuchins across town using only a hand truck. Capuchins are easily excited, so Dave's boss, Jim, thought it best to move them this way. Holes were punched in the sides of the box and moving tape sealed the top as he began to move them across town.

The capuchins were making a ridiculous racket as Dave waited for the light to change at 42nd Street and 7th Avenue. A beautiful blonde in a white cotton dress and sandals smiled at Dave as they stood together on the corner.

"Whatcha got in the box?" she asked as a capuchin finger poked out from one of the air holes in the box.

"Monkeys," Dave replied. "Capuchin monkeys. I move monkeys for a living."

"You do not! No one does that. Can I see one?" The odd conversation made the young woman seem somewhat flirtatious in her attitude. Dave could not resist.

"Sure. Look through the air holes." The capuchins were revved up.

She peered into the side of the box and could see live monkey parts but nary a whole monkey anywhere. "Unbelievable! It's kinda hard to see them like this, though. Could you open the top?" She pulled on Dave's shirt sleeve and smiled broadly.

Dave knew it was against the rules and that time was a wastin'. He needed to deliver his monkeys, but the underlying sexual tension of this encounter was driving him insane. He hesitated only for a moment;

surely, it couldn't hurt for this woman to have a quick look. Carefully, he opened the top, but it was as if the capricious capuchin was waiting for him. Before Dave could realize what was happening, the monkey jumped out of the box, over his shoulders, and onto the street to the intermingled horror and great joy of the young woman and the surrounding bystanders.

The monkey broke towards the traffic. Seeing that its own death was imminent due to the approaching flock of flying steel vehicles, it veered back towards Dave and the young lady. She started laughing hysterically as Dave feverishly worked to close the box and imprison the remaining monkeys while he reached out to capture the one who got away.

A buxom woman wearing a tight, brown shirt screamed in horror as the capuchin leapt up on her chest seeking a springboard to freedom. She fell backwards as she fainted and hit her head on a parked car.

Having secured the other monkeys, Dave ran down the street shouting at the escapee, imploring bystanders to help him. The horror and laughter of all who were witness to the great chase rippled down the street as the monkey scrambled up a restaurant awning, leapt onto a fire escape ladder, and climbed to the roof of a small apartment building.

Dave sat on the curb for a moment, sweating and out of breath, not sure what he should do next. Only one monkey had escaped. He looked down the street and saw that the woman he'd left behind was still with his other monkeys—apparently doubled over with laughter.

A police car roared down the street with its siren on and another approached the corner as Dave walked back to his monkeys. He wiped the sweat off of his brow and saw a crowd of people speaking with the police and pointing to him as he approached. The girl he'd met on the corner was not laughing anymore.

"These your monkeys?" the police officer asked officiously.

"Yeah." Dave sounded deflated and depressed. "They are my monkeys."

"You got a permit to transfer them around the city?"

"Right here," Dave said as he pulled it out of his pocket. "I'm supposed to bring them to the behavioral sciences lab at the university. One just got away."

"Behavioral sciences lab?" The blonde woman looked horrified. "What are you—some kind of monkey Mengele? How can you hurt these poor little guys?" She began to back away. "And to think I thought you were cute!"

"It isn't me," Dave said. "It's the scientists. They hook up all these cathodes to them and see how they react to different types of stimuli."

The policeman looked at Dave. "Let's focus here, son. You say one got away? Which way did it go?"

"It's on the roof of that apartment building." Dave pointed towards the middle of the street. "It won't hurt anyone. They just eat fruit. Loose in the city, it is much more likely to be scared of the people and devoured by rats."

The policeman directed his associates to the apartment building to go "monkey hunting." He radioed animal control. "Now, you and me are going to deliver these monkeys nice and fast, and then we'll come back to help find the other one. Got it?"

Dave nodded as he loaded the monkeys and himself into the van driven by one of the other patrolmen. There were derisive chants of "monkey boy" and "ape man" hurled at him by the crowd that had assembled around the excitement. Someone even tossed a banana into Dave's lap as he sat in the van.

Dave had never felt more foolish or embarrassed in his life. The worst part of this fiasco was that, for the first time in a very, very long time, a woman had found him "interesting and cute"—and within fifteen minutes he had become a monkey-hating Nazi in her eyes. Why did I ever take this job? he wondered as the cop drove him to the lab.

By the end of the day, animal control had caught the rogue monkey. The police had given Dave a summons for the illegal release of a jungle animal within city limits. The lab had fired Dave for all the negative publicity he had brought to them and their work. The evening news had shown footage of Dave, the girl, and the escaped monkey. It turned out that the entire imbroglio had transpired in front of a TV studio, and local news had captured most everything on tape.

Dave sat in his apartment in front of the TV watching himself chase a capuchin monkey down Seventh Avenue for the tenth time in a row. He held his head in his left hand and an empty beer can in his right. Dave had never felt so low in his life. Friends were calling and leaving monkey sounds for messages, asking for "monkey boy," or wondering about what it was like to be a star.

He could never look his friends in the eye again without knowing that they were laughing at him behind his back. And he could never return to Gabe's Bar again. Sally had already mocked him about his job— what would she think of him now? The tears began to flow as Dave thought about how far his life had fallen.

It was time to move. Maybe if he moved far enough away, he could leave his past behind and start his life over. He decided that it was the only chance he had. He began to pack. Anything that reminded him of the past would be left behind. Anyone who knew him at any time in the past would be dropped from his social/business calendars. Dave was determined to start anew.

• • •

Sheila took the scissors and frenetically moved from picture to picture in her apartment. She would take a picture from its frame, cut out her image, and return the picture to its frame again. If Ed had no way to determine how beautiful "old Sheila" had been, he'd never be turned off by the overweight, mole-studded, large-handed version of the "new Sheila." Ed would fall for her, and they would be married and live happily ever after. The plan was flawless. She smiled at her "nick of time" brilliance. All would be ready for Ed tomorrow night.

Photo albums! Family photo albums. Sheila almost forgot. Imagine if Ed had seen them and asked to glimpse Sheila's past! Scissors in hand, Sheila ran to her closet and began to cut.

By midnight, her room was awash in old picture parts and the history of Sheila. By one a.m., she had gathered all the pieces and placed them in a dark green garbage bag. She put on a T-shirt and shorts and took the bag out to the Dumpster. The exorcism of old Sheila was now complete, and new Sheila was tired but satisfied. Her hands hurt from all the cutting, and a blister was beginning to form on her right thumb, but she was free! She jumped into bed—ecstatic that the transformation was complete, euphoric that she had thought of the idea in the first place, and confident that tomorrow was going to be a special night with Ed.

Sheila shrieked as she was about to put her head upon the pillow. One more family picture lurked, hidden on the second shelf of her night table. Exhausted from hours of cutting and collecting, she picked up the picture and threw it, frame and all, into the garbage pail. That garbage would have to go out on Saturday afternoon. She thanked God for allowing her to catch that picture before Ed came over.

It was a beautiful day on Saturday. Sheila was beyond excited about her date with Ed. She went to the beauty parlor and fixed as many body parts and hair follicles as she could. She bought a slinky silk dress that had a girdle-like device sewn into its sides so that she would look slimmer. She decided that she would wear no undergarments that night. She hoped that, if she felt sexy, she would be sexy, and Ed would think her appealing and sexy.

She sat on a red felt-covered chair as she waited for Ed. It was 7:30 and she was reviewing every part of her body as she waited.

At eight, her doorbell rang.

"Nice place." Ed seemed genuinely impressed. "I love the way you have it set up."

Sheila's smile was broad as it could be. She had never been so happy in her life. Her eyes glistened under too much mascara, and she giggled nervously.

"Whoa! What happened here?" Ed was looking at the gaping hole in the large family picture.

Sheila's opalescent cheeks blushed red suddenly and sweat began to form between her nose and lip. She didn't really know what to say.

"That...that is my family." Sheila was beginning to question the wisdom of her plan of the prior evening. "I cut myself out because I looked absolutely dreadful in that picture. But my family looked great, so I wanted to keep it."

Ed looked at Sheila slowly. He was trying to control his facial expressions and maintain an even demeanor despite the fact that he thought Sheila's explanation completely bizarre.

Sheila reached for her shawl and threw it over her shoulder. "Maybe we should go now. It is past eight and we have to make the movie after dinner."

"Yes." Ed was speaking in an absent-minded tone as his gaze took him around the apartment filled with pictures that had misplaced gaps in each.

He looked at Sheila differently, or so she thought. "Are you the one missing from all of these photos?"

Sheila smiled sheepishly. "Well, yes."

"Why did you hang them all up if you looked so bad in them that you felt the need to cut them?"

This was a question that didn't have a good answer. Sheila's eyes teared slightly as she responded. "I'm just a bit strange about photos, I guess." Sweat was flowing from all of her pores. Her stomach ached. She felt like a fool.

An absent-minded "yes" escaped from Ed's mouth as he continued to look around the apartment. He looked at Sheila and then he looked at his watch again. It was Ed's turn to be uncomfortable.

"You know, Sheila. I don't feel very well. Long flight and all, it must be catching up to me. Maybe a rain check for tonight?"

Sheila was on the verge of hysterics. She asked Ed if he just wanted to stay at her place for a while to see if he felt better after a time. They could skip the movie.

Ed grew more unconsciously adamant in his response. "No, I really think I've got to go. I'll call you, I promise." Ed quickly kissed Sheila on the cheek, moved to the door, and left. Sheila ran to her bedroom and threw herself on the covers. How could she have been so stupid? How could she be so crazy? How could she ever face Ed or anyone else in this town again? Sheila cried long and hard into the night.

• • •

The first time Francis put on the clothes he had stolen from his mother's closet, he felt foolish and awkward. He had locked his bedroom door and moved some furniture in front of it so that no one could possibly get in. He loved the silky feel of the clothes against his body. It made him feel aroused, but when he looked in the mirror, he was depressed.

Due to differences in size and basic anatomy, his mother's clothes did not fit him the way he had hoped. They had the wonderful fragrance of his mother, but he looked silly and out of place in them. He rubbed her silky nightgown all over his body, and that made him feel better. He felt special. He tried putting on makeup, and he felt better still.

Gradually, Francis became more adept at the purchase of women's clothes and the styling of his body, closer and closer to that "perfect presence" he wanted to show the world. Different than his mother's idea of "perfect," but "ironically perfect" to him.

He kept a bag of clothing, makeup, and wigs with him at all times. When the mood struck, he'd sneak to a bathroom or an abandoned parking lot to become the "Fran" he could live with, his new face to the outside world.

Over time, Francis found other men like himself and began to hang out in places that only they would know. His life became an odd combination of strange sexual relationships and beatings. His conversations and attitudes moved away from normal and mainstream as he got deeper into his lifestyle.

His mom knew something was wrong, of course, but was not really interested in doing anything about it. She watched her son leave her behind emotionally and did nothing. She decided to focus on her own life and happiness and spent less and less time with Francis. To her, it had become obvious that Francis had too much of his father's DNA to be worth any more effort from her. There were those who were beyond help. There were those who refused help. To make the effort to help those people was, to her, a fool's errand that she did not wish to undertake. It would be easier to ignore his existence than to become involved in his recovery.

She never knew it, but Francis often sneaked into her room at night. He enjoyed watching her sleep, hoping that her covers would come off so he could see her entire body. He used to mimic some of her sleep poses and buy the same lingerie if he thought it attractive. Sometimes he caressed the clothing in her closet as he watched her sleep, and more than once he wondered what it would be like to make love to her.

• • •

Dave grew a beard and headed for Florida. He never spoke of his past to anyone. When asked, he would deflect the questions with stories of his journeys from outer space or something equally preposterous. People thought him odd. He lived in a small town where everyone knew everyone and no one felt that they knew him. Actually, no one even wanted to get to know him. Dave felt disconsolate, detached, and alone.

• • •

Sheila woke up Sunday morning wearing the dress she had put on for Ed the night before. She looked at herself in the mirror—mascara was all over her face, her hair was a tangled mess, and her dress had ridden up her body, exposing her fat and unsightly thighs. She ripped her dress off and threw it in the corner.

She ran to her closet and pulled at her travel bags. She was not going to spend another minute in this town. She was beaten and ashamed. She began to pack her bags with a vengeance. South, she said without thinking. I'm going to head south.

• • •

In the end, Francis enjoyed the life of a quasi-prostitute more than his own. He never had a genuine conversation, but all of the lust and the love seemed so real. There were times he realized that he had never had a true relationship with another human being, and that caused him to feel great sadness. Still, he always knew that he would never again feel the pain of the patio of his youth. He would never again see the pity reserved for the hopeless in the eyes of another. The consolation of knowing that he would never experience such pain again was adequate compensation for the lack of emotional relationships in his life.

After he left her, his mother used the story of her wayward and missing son to position herself as the loving victim of a boy gone wrong. This helped her to meet a rich, handsome man who was almost as vacuous as she. They married and never really cared for each other for the rest of their lives, enjoying their world of blessed excess together.

• • •

Dick Starke was the coroner and funeral director of a tiny town in North Florida called Spring. Dick had grown up in Spring, gone to school in Spring, and returned to Spring after he completed his studies at the University of Florida.

Dick wore silver-rimmed glasses and had a bushy white walrus mustache. He had grown fat over the years, and his ample belly extended a good foot over his belt. He was the best-dressed man in town. He always wore a suit and a tie because he thought that his jobs called for it. His best friends, Ray and Stevie, whom he'd known since grade school, often got drunk at the local bar and told all who would listen that the reason Dick was so well-dressed was that he would take the clothes off of the corpses before he buried them—who would ever know? It was the perfect crime.

Dick would laugh along with them and shake his head in a dismissive way. He said that that was the way of Ray and Stevie, always with the crude humor. Still, he did have a lot of suits, and no one saw him at the department store very often.

Today, Dick had gotten called in on a serious set of cases. Three apparent suicides—two Jane Does and a John Doe. They'd all slashed their own throats, right down to the voice box. They'd all done it in the bathrooms of their rented apartments. They all were found within an hour of each other, yet no one in Spring knew any of them.

The last point bothered Dick a lot. You'd have to try pretty hard to be anonymous in Spring. Coincidence? He thought...maybe. A coincidence is where two completely unrelated events appear to be alike. Usually, there is more that is dissimilar than similar to any coincidence. How on earth were these three related?

The pale white light of a November sunset streamed through the windows and fell on the floor.

The bodies laid on the table were lined up before Dick, dressed in the blood-soaked clothes in which they had been found. The white light had a curious effect on Dick and on the appearance of the room. This was a sad tableau at the end of time. Everything looked so old. Dick felt the ponderous nature of the setting sun that made him consider his own mortality as he approached the dead trio before him.

Dick took off his glasses and rubbed his eyes hard before he started. Little old ladies who died of natural causes he could deal with; young people who sliced their own throats were quite another story.

He paused again before he began. Why in the world did I decide to do this for a living? There were so many other things I could have done, he thought.

He began to undress the victims. Hmmm. Make that two John Does and one Jane Doe.

This was a day filled with firsts for the town of Spring and Dick Starke.

He began to perform the autopsies. A small tear formed at the corner of his eye.

"I really don't like this," he said to no one, "but what am I to do? I am the coroner of Spring. I am the funeral director of Spring. The people here need me to be these things."

For some reason, the sight of these young dead bodies had a great effect on Dick. He stopped working for a moment and looked out the window as the sun set and the townspeople of Spring went about their limited business.

He thought about Rodney Miller. Dick shook his head slightly. He had known Rodney since they were in the seventh grade. By the time they were seniors in high school, he was drinking quite heavily. By the time he was thirty, he was a raging alcoholic trapped by his view of himself as the town "party boy." He died when he was fifty.

Dick picked up his glasses for a moment to resume his work when he began to think about Mark Cranston. Every day, for many years, Mark had slung the hash at the Spring Inn grill to support his wife and two kids. He hated his job; eventually he hated the responsibilities that were thrust upon him by his family. He had nowhere to go, no hope to succeed. He ate his shotgun on Super Bowl Sunday, and Dick stood remembering that autopsy like it happened just yesterday.

Dick rubbed his left eye with his left hand and spoke to no one in particular once again. "Everyone is without hope. Everyone will die without redemption. Some people play out the string; others get frustrated, upset, and end it early by living badly or committing a quicker, more efficient suicide."

His attention then returned to the bodies before him. A young man, a young woman, a transvestite all dead before him in the town of Spring—an unbelievable coincidence, hadn't seen something like this in town—EVER.

"Why am I the coroner of Spring anyway?" A dark smile creased his face as his hand moved towards his glasses.

"I guess I like my suicides slow." Dick put on his glasses and got to work.

The Waters of San Sebastiano

One hundred twenty-one people died constructing the Cathedral of San Sebastiano. This number was greater than the town's population between the years 863 and 1444. When it was at a cosmopolitan zenith in the 1830s, San Sebastiano was a town of approximately 218 people, 215 of whom were Catholics. The people of the town attended church every Sunday and had an almost superstitious belief in the power of God. Everyone in town stopped by the cathedral to pray at least once a week. The three people in town who were not Catholic attended Mass at the Cathedral of San Sebastiano every Christmas and Easter. The solemn beauty of the ceremony was always quite compelling to all.

San Sebastiano had always been a fishing town tucked, as it was, into a small elbow of the Mediterranean Sea. Her people enjoyed the sea and felt a strong psychic connection to its ways. The cathedral, which had been finished in October of 1736, had remained relatively unchanged since the day that it opened. The large grey bricks that had been hoisted into place and set by skilled artisans of another era were now black with age. The large oaken doors that provided entrance to the cathedral were still locked by a slide bolt beam that had been put into place every evening by the church pastor for more than 250 years.

Beside the church (which was the cultural and spiritual center of the town), and facing the sea, was a cemetery that seemed to exist in spite of the burgeoning signs of progress that surrounded it. An elaborate Gothic gate stood at its entrance. Leaning against the gate, partially shaded by a tall cypress tree, was a blind man in rags mindlessly gnawing on the top of his right wrist.

Inside the gate, oddly shaped tombstones, some barely legible, leaned at acute and obtuse angles in uneven rows, planted as they were at different times in the history of the town. Only Catholics were buried in this cemetery. Any non-Catholic who died in San Sebastiano was given a brief civil ceremony and then brought out to sea to be food for the fish that were the commercial basis for the town. It was a policy that had worked for hundreds of years. Now, the graveyard was full and it fell to a modern-day pastor to decide what should become of the remains of those long dead and recently deceased.

Whether you were a Catholic who believed that a body was resurrected and delivered to heaven after a good life and a short death, or a Catholic who believed that only the well-mannered soul was delivered to heaven while its house, the earthly body, remained behind, you knew that the pastor was struggling on the horns of a dilemma with which no good man should have to deal. In lighter moments, he considered piling the recently deceased atop the old and now dusty remains. It was his grim sense of the macabre that allowed these thoughts to enter his mind.

The window of the pastor's office overlooked the graveyard. Every day he looked at the crowd of disheveled dead before him. Every day he looked at the poorly ordered rows bordered by ancient cypress, wondering what he was going to do.

Pastor Pietro Renato took off the half-glasses he used for reading and tossed them onto a small stack of papers that sat on the desk before him. The new addition to his office was humming too loudly beside him, and he looked at it with a mixture of disdain and dismay. The electronic vision of St. Peter's Basilica was striking in its beauty, but Pietro found the computer's noise, as well as its capacity for connection and information from around the world, completely out of place in the fishing hamlet of San Sebastiano. On the shore, villagers repaired nets that had been used for years and years while Renato's computer received three more blasted updates from the College of Cardinals regarding the church's position on issues that would always be irrelevant to the people of San Sebastiano.

The priest massaged his eyes with his thumb and forefinger and let his hand fall to scrub his nose, cheeks, and chin. It was a glorious day, the wind whispered by his open window, and birds sang from the branches of the trees that bordered the cemetery. The deep silence of the church and the cemetery provided stark contrast to the activity of the small town now waking to a new day. Gazing upon the magnificence of the day before him, Renato contemplated great beauty and perfect days.

He had a problem with earthly beauty. He realized that all goodness came from the Lord, but that did not mean that he could easily appreciate beauty beyond this rather broad and distant view. He remembered reading a line in a book whose plot he had long forgotten: "Happiness is never grand." It was a line that resonated with Renato beyond its creative worthiness. Not only was happiness not grand, earthly happiness was not important at all. How could one revel in the transient beauty of an earthly day when there was only true beauty and perfection in the afterlife? Why should one be emotionally challenged to enjoy a nice day when God's perfection could also be witnessed in thunder, wind, and rain? How does one enjoy himself in a world so seriously flawed?

Renato's musings were interrupted by a knock on his door and a lighthearted voice calling his name. "Pietro! Pietro Renato! I know you are in there. You cannot ignore me. I will not go away."

Pietro smiled as he rose to answer the door. It was the call of his old friend, Jude, who had promised to visit Renato that day.

"Patience, Jude, patience. I was working, deep in thought. I will be with you in a moment." Renato pushed himself away from his desk and moved toward the door to let in his friend. Renato had been looking forward to this visit.

A broad smile was on Jude's face as he held out his hands to Renato. "Pietro, how are you? Isn't it a glorious day? You should be outside enjoying the day like everyone else." Jude surveyed Pietro's office with mock disdain. "Well, isn't this plush? Quite a descent from that palatial office in Madrid, hmmm? Oh, but you have a computer and an image of St. Peter's. How wonderful!"

"Perhaps Father Jude should be more concerned with piety and less with the vile materialism of a secular world." Renato smiled as he admonished him. "Seriously, it is quiet and it is slow, but it is nice all the same. Perhaps I do not have the elevated trappings or majestic position I had in Madrid, but I feel more like a priest again."

Jude's face changed as he listened to Pietro speak. The smile faded from his face as he felt concern for his friend overtake him. "One incident. One lousy incident. I feel for you, my friend."

For a moment, a look of extreme anger passed across Pietro's face. "We will not speak of it. It did not happen, Jude. You are my friend. You should know. It never happened." His voice was little more than a whisper as he spoke, and his eyes locked onto Jude's with an unwavering glare.

Jude held his hands up as a sign of peace. "I believe you, my friend, I believe you. I was just expressing my frustration over the fact that others did not. We will speak no more of it. The day is too bright for such a dark subject." He smiled as he searched his friend's face for a crack that did not contain anger so he could break the seal. Jude wanted to return his friend's demeanor to its prior, relaxed state.

Pietro finally relented. "Let's sit outside and have some tea. We can try to enjoy this glorious day about which you keep waxing lyrical. Maria, Maria. *Caffè* on the porch, please."

A voice from a source unseen penetrated the hallway as the men left Renato's office. "In a moment, pastor. I'll be with you in a moment."

"Servants, too?" Jude smiled and winked at his friend. "This *is* plush!"

"Relax, Jude. Relax. Maria came with the church. She is a very sweet young lady who has lived a very troubled life. She is very bright; very, very bright. A woman of great capability in a town that only appreciates the quality of the catch. How does such a woman live here? Her brothers treat her like a slave, her father is no better. She waits on them hand and foot every day without a moment to herself. She has no self-respect. She has nothing. The sad thing is that she believes what her family tells her. She believes she can do no better. To me, this is tragic."

"How do you know so much, Renato? You can't care that much; she is your servant, too." Jude loved to challenge his friend.

"Don't speak to me of that, Jude. I have been trying to help her. I often counsel her. I do what I can to help her feel special. I do everything that I can…" Renato's voice trailed off as Maria approached.

Within a few moments of their taking their seats, a young woman brought a tray with two cups of *caffè*, and sugar, to the priests. Maria did not lean over to serve the priests but instead lowered her body to the level of the table with a deliberate formality and placed the contents of her tray before them. She wore a puffy white blouse with red piping around the gathered sleeves and neckline. Her red jumper was belted tightly around her waist but fell loosely away from her body, creating a relaxed appearance that was further accentuated by her leather sandals. To Jude, she appeared to be in her late twenties or early thirties. Her long chestnut hair was extremely curly and drawn together in a long ponytail that fell to the middle of her back. She made the sign of the cross after she served them.

It was only when Renato thanked her that she finally looked up. Meeting his eyes, Maria smiled broadly, revealing perfect white teeth. Jude thought he caught a hint of perfume also. Though a priest, the sight of a perfectly formed body did not miss his attention.

When he felt that Maria was far enough away, Jude finally spoke. "Do you feel that resisting temptation gets you a better seat in heaven?"

Renato, whose mind had been elsewhere, was roused by Jude's question. "What in the world are you speaking about, Jude?"

Jude's face took on a positively earthly demeanor as he spoke and pointed to the passageway to which Maria had just returned. "You know..." Here he directed his head to the passageway for emphasis. "Maria."

Renato rolled his eyes and looked at his friend with incredulity. "Why did you become a priest? I swear that, at times, you've got the mind and spiritual compass of a lounge singer."

"I meant nothing by it. Unlike you, I appreciate the beauty that surrounds us. This is all God's creation, you know. His majesty is everywhere. As a priest, how can you ignore it?"

Cryptically, Renato replied, "It is all God's creation until it is not. Then what?"

Missing Renato's point, Jude replied, "That is where we come in, my friend. That is our job."

Renato dismissed Jude's response with a wave of his hand and returned to his drink. The two men finished their *caffè* in silence, each appreciating the beauty of the day in his own way.

Finally, Renato relented and broke the silence. "Come, I have a problem here. I would like to discuss it with you and see what you think."

The men rose from their chairs. Jude smiled and gently placed his hand on the middle of his friend's back as they walked. "What is it, Renato? How can I help?"

It was in that moment that Renato felt the value of his long friendship with Jude. Jude was maddening, of course. At times, he was an absolute enigma to Renato. Renato could not reconcile the priest with the man. Still, beneath it all, Jude was a good man who could be relied upon to help whenever Renato needed him. Through so many moments in his life, through so many changes, Renato did not know how it would have all turned out without his friend Jude. Jude's faith in him was unique when Renato needed him most. He had stood beside him in Spain. He believed in him when no one else did. Renato always remembered that it was Jude who held his shoulders and told him that he would always stand beside him. Jude's love for Renato was unconditional.

Renato continued to eye the ground before him, noticing the dust that was stirred from the surface of the paths and the unsightly weeds that bordered it. Weeds always seemed to grow in the least arable places without anyone to care for them while the most meticulously maintained garden or grass would fail on a regular basis.

The faint scent of dead fish was borne along the path by the thin wind, which was constantly present in a town filled with aged constancies. Because they were not yet close enough, the shouting of the fishermen as they barked lamentations and commands at each other seemed like the background music of a town. A town which ran at the beat of a tired laborer unconsciously trying to reconcile the hope that is the motivating factor of all who fish with the quiet fatalism of a life that would not venture far beyond the five square miles that made up the surface area of the town.

Jude had put on his favorite pair of sunglasses and was surveying the activity on the shore, and the seabirds that screeched and dove for fish. As the two men drew closer to the water, the scent of the sea and the fish grew.

Jude turned to Pietro. "You have much to love here." The sound of Jude's voice eased Renato from the depth of his thought and brought him back to the world before him. "I am sorry. What did you say? My mind was elsewhere."

Jude surveyed Pietro's appearance with great concern and inquisition. Too often, it seemed to him that his friend was somewhere else when he was beside him. "There is much to love here. The simple beauty of this place has the power to overwhelm in a quiet, peaceful way. Many say there is great peace in tranquility. I disagree. I believe the peaceful tranquility of a place like this can sometimes be too much. The greatest majesty of God's creation does not only exist in grand acts and dynamic landscapes. The seductive power of perfect creation where peace reinvents itself every day in the face of undying evil is, to me, a greater example of God's perfect love for his creation."

For a moment, the pastor thought that he should stop their walk so that he could embrace his friend and apologize for his "lounge singer" crack. This was what Renato loved about Jude. At any moment, he could take a simple event and infuse it with the power of the almighty. He could take a mundane statement and turn it into a thought more profound. It was at these times Renato realized that, in spite of all the feelings of "liturgical superiority" he had when he was with Jude, he knew that Jude was the better man and the better priest.

Renato smiled and placed his hand on Jude's shoulder. "You are a fine man and a vigilant priest. When faced with the sublime on earth, you see the eternal battle between good and evil and the transcendent superiority of good. Others have said that evil is best characterized as an unlidded eye surrounded by flame bending the will of souls otherwise good to a wicked path of self-destruction. Instead, you see the silent power of an almighty good that overwhelms, with its subtlety, the everlasting simplicity and constancy that eventually destroy the apparent value of mutability to the masses. These fish were always here. These fishermen were always here—the size of the catch and the color of the boat mean so little." Renato continued to smile as he squinted in the bright sunlight. Unconsciously, he nodded his head as his gaze returned to the shell dust on the path before him.

Again, Jude placed his hand on Pietro's back. "What is it, Renato? What troubles you on this glorious day?"

"The living…and the dead. I don't know what to do about them."

Jude paused to evaluate his friend and interpret his meaning before he spoke. "Again, that is our job, isn't it? Determining what to do with the living and helping to deliver the dead to a promised land of perfect happiness and eternal salvation?"

Pietro smiled when he realized that Jude was unable to decipher what he really meant. Still, a playful side of his character drove him to continue the charade for a few more moments. "All the living die. Is that not true, Jude?"

"Yes, my friend, it is," Jude replied, still wondering where this conversation was headed.

"And the dead will be delivered to heaven. The kind and forgiving God of the everlasting will accept them and forgive their earthly sins?"

"Yes, as long as they are truly remorseful." Jude was beginning to think that Renato had been in the sun too long.

"Well, then, what can I do with the living who become dead?"

"Bury them and pray for their salvation."

"But I don't have the room…. Look." Pietro pointed past the blind beggar with the bandage wrapped around his head who slept beside the Gothic gate at the cemetery entrance. "I have nowhere to put them anymore. My cemetery is almost full. Where can I put the living when they die? Where do I put the dead, long gone? What can I do?"

Finally realizing that his friend was posing a legitimate question in a curiously coquettish way, Jude rubbed his chin and said, "Dig deeper graves and pile them one atop the other?"

"Water table too high," Renato said.

"Mausoleums for the newly dead?"

"Too modern. The townspeople would never accept it."

"New land, somewhere else? New cemetery?"

"This is where the dead live. They live in the cemetery of the Cathedral of San Sebastiano. They cannot live elsewhere."

"How many die each year? How much room do you need?"

Renato was a bit taken aback by the antiseptic mathematics of the question posed by his friend, but he thought for a moment and responded. "Six to ten per year, I think. But this year, there are some that cross the century mark. This has never happened before. It might be a banner year for the dead." Renato smiled as he surveyed the fishermen working their boats, looking for sickly candidates.

Jude surveyed the land around the church, the walls and gates of the cemetery, and the blind beggar who was spitting on the path where Pietro Renato had just walked.

"This wall needs repair, especially back there." Jude pointed to a corner of the graveyard where the wall was crumbling. Outside the wall, the blossoms of a beautiful fruit tree were dropping to the ground at the hint of wind that whispered past the graves. "Why not knock down the wall, cut out the fruit tree behind it, and rebuild the wall there by the base of that grassy knoll? Consecrate the land, and you are open for business again. It will take some time, but just be sure that your town elders continue to live and to eat well. The dead will have a place to live for years to come, and you'll be gone before this problem rears its ugly head once more."

In the face of Jude's cold pragmatism, Renato's face grew ashen. "What's wrong now?" asked Jude.

"Maria loves the fruit of that tree," he whispered. "When I first arrived, she shared some of it with me." Pietro Renato was visibly wistful as he recalled the day, the fruit, and Maria. It seemed so long ago.

Jude was preoccupied with his re-engineering plan for the dead of San Sebastiano. "Good fruit? Well, then, transplant the tree."

"Yes. Yes. We can do that." The pastor's attention had gone to some other place, some other time. He was there again and was not.

"Or maybe not." Jude spoke these words with a volume and gusto that roused Pietro Renato from his reverie. "Pietro…what is it? At times today, I have felt like I was talking to myself. You are so distracted, so distant."

Pietro Renato was visibly shaken. He wanted to deflect Jude's attention, but he didn't know how. Renato lived in a world where he was mostly alone and aloof, separated from those around him by his position, involved with them only through religion. He tried to change the subject. "It is nothing, my friend. It really is nothing at all. I must consider your suggestion. In the meantime, let's forget my problems and speak about you. How is your mother? Are your brothers and sisters well?" Renato knew that Jude loved to speak about his family, and he was relatively certain that his line of questioning would refocus Jude's attention.

Once again, Jude eyed his troubled friend from beneath his sunglasses. Once again, he saw a man who had not embraced the peace of this town. He felt that his friend was sharing an embrace with thoughts inappropriate, but he did not know how to persuade him to reveal his problem. Realizing that penetrating the seal of Pietro Renato when he resisted was an exercise in futility, he decided that some lighthearted conversation might bring his friend out of himself. Jude had seen Renato in a state of mind very similar to this many times before. At one moment, Renato could be brooding and pensive; five minutes later he could be motivated to great happiness. When Renato was this way, all of his moods were short lived.

The two men approached the shoreline deep in a lighthearted conversation that involved the shopping habits of Jude's ninety-year-old mother. Pietro Renato laughed and smiled as they walked. The conversation had removed him from the troubles that were the parish of San Sebastiano and allowed him to feel as happy as he had been in quite some time.

At the water's edge, deeply tanned fishermen with curly black hair and thick mustaches barked commands to young men who were learning their trade and the difficulties one can encounter when fishing with five nets. Jude had just told Renato about his mother's belief that the hot water faucet exists on the left side of the sink because the left hand is the hand of the devil, when one of the young fishermen approached the priest with a large, live fish in his hands.

"Padre, padre." He nodded to both priests as he spoke. "This fish is good fish. Good dinner fish. We want to give it to you." The young man nodded respectfully and smiled as he finished his sentence.

Renato eyed the fish somewhat suspiciously as Jude clapped his hands enthusiastically. Jude was smiling broadly. "I love fresh fish. Could we have it tonight, Renato? Do we have other plans for dinner?"

Renato smiled at the fisherman and then less broadly at his friend, Jude. Not wanting to insult the fisherman or disappoint Jude, he accepted the fish graciously. Still, he wanted to continue to walk and talk with Jude, so he looked at the fisherman and asked for a favor. "Presario, my friend, could you bring the fish to the church now and give it to a woman there named Maria? Please ask her to prepare it for a seven o'clock meal that Father Jude and I will share."

Presario smiled very broadly indeed. It was great good luck to have a priest accept a portion of the catch; to use it as dinner for a special friend who was also a priest was an honor beyond his wildest dreams. This would mean a great catch tomorrow.

"Maria??!! She is my cousin's sister-in-law! I will take it to her, Padre, I will take it right now!" The dark brown fish quietly gasped its last few breaths as its gills were crushed by the enthusiastic grasp of the excited young fisherman.

Though he was happy at the prospect of a lucky day and a great catch the next day, the thought of visiting Maria brought something else to mind. "Padre Renato. Before I go to Maria, I must tell you that it may be dangerous for her to cook this fish for you. Maria is very sick. I don't want you to be sick if you eat fish cooked by her. Maybe I should have my wife cook it instead?" Having died in his hands, the fish's eyes were hardened and dry. It made no movement in his hand.

Renato was concerned about how religion and superstition were interchangeable in San

Sebastiano. He always spoke against it whenever he saw superstition in practice. He wanted the people to believe in the existence, providence, and power of God. Renato believed that it would be good for him to have more devout believers, for them to believe in the almighty nature of the Lord their God and in Mother Church. "You speak in crazy ways, my friend. Maria is not sick. I've seen her every day this week."

"My cousin tells me Maria is sick every morning. Every day for over a month now, very bad."

Renato examined the fisherman; there was no lie in him. Still, Pietro Renato did not believe Maria was sick. He definitely did not believe that any sickness she might have would be transmitted to them through the consumption of a dead fish. "It's no problem. Do not trouble your wife. Please bring the fish to Maria to prepare."

"I will go right now, Padre. Thank you, thank you."

"No, my friend," Renato was smiling now. "It is I who should be thanking you." Renato watched the fisherman as he began his journey toward the church, dead fish in hand.

"What a curious little man," said Jude. "He seemed so anxious to serve you well. Places great stock in the satisfaction of a priest, he does. I can't wait for dinner."

Renato shook his head. "Right now, I am concerned about Maria. She did not seem like she was sick to me today. Did she look ill to you?"

Jude smiled. "She looked perfectly fine to me. Do not worry, Pietro. I am sure that our excitable little fisherman is mistaken."

Renato shrugged. "Perhaps you are right, my friend. I could be worried about nothing—for no reason at all." His brow was furrowed, and he attempted to divert his friend's attention to the small fishing boats that dotted the waterscape before them.

They walked along the shore until sunset. At times, they engaged in conversation about their brothers in the priesthood; at times, they walked in silence. As they approached the church, they could smell fish cooking.

"After a long walk and long conversation, there is nothing like a hot meal and a few glasses of wine." Jude grasped his ample belly and shook it for emphasis.

Maria had set a smart table. She filled large glasses with a local red wine and began to bring in plates of vegetables and potatoes for the men. Finally, the star of the feast arrived, freshly broiled and wrapped in a scent of slight garlic.

Jude cut into the fish, removed its head, and tossed it into an empty bowl with the deftness of an experienced fisherman. He then deboned the fish in seconds while Pietro Renato looked on in amazement.

"You never cease to amaze. Just when I think that I have uncovered your best thought and greatest talents, you show me something new, something I never thought that you could do." For a moment, Renato felt an unencumbered joy, a feeling that he had not felt in years.

Jude slammed the knife into the wooden table for emphasis. "Not only a fisher of men am I, Pietro Renato. At one time, I, too, was fisherman. We all know how to filet!"

Both men laughed and drained their glasses. As Jude refilled them and placed the empty bottle on the table, Maria returned with a new one.

Looking at the ground as she spoke, Maria addressed both men. "I hope that all is satisfactory. Is there anything else that you need?"

Between forkfuls of asparagus, potatoes, and fish, Jude exclaimed that everything was perfect, but before he let her go, he had to ask one question. Maria paused, lifted her eyes to look at the fat priest, and waited for his question.

"How do you feel, Maria? Are you well?"

For a moment, Maria blushed bright red and then she recovered. "I am fine, Father. Thank you for asking." Jude waved absentmindedly as his attention returned to his food.

Maria nodded her head slightly and moved to leave as Pietro Renato held up his hand to stop her. Without raising her head or her eyes, Maria stopped for an instant. "After dinner, I'd like to see you in my office, Maria. There is something I'd like to speak with you about. Will you come and see me then?"

"Yes, Father," Maria said, her eyes still averted. "I will be there." Maria walked quickly out of the room.

Jude looked at Pietro Renato as he chewed a mouthful of food. Swallowing, he said, "Why do you worry so? She is fine!"

Renato stared at his friend for a moment. "It's what I do. I can't help but worry."

After a few plates full of food and a small dessert, Jude declared himself satisfied. He was tired from their walk. Jude graciously thanked Renato and retired to bed. He promised that, in the morning, he would help Renato solve the mystery of what to do with the dead.

Feeling a bit light-headed from the wine, Renato sat and watched as Maria cleared the dishes and cleaned the table for a few minutes. Finally, he got up and told her that he would be waiting for her in his office. Maria nodded and continued to clean.

Renato stared out of his window into the empty blackness that consumed the town at night. There were small sounds of nature and the intermittent shuffling of the blind beggar as he approached the kitchen window to receive the leftover vegetables from Maria. Renato was now quite sad and worried about so many things: the living, the dying, the dead. He could find no solace in things worldly.

Finally, Maria approached his door and knocked lightly. He asked her to come in. The beggar sat beneath the priest's window to eat. He had heard the priest in his room as he wandered looking for a place to sit and eat. The beggar felt less lonely when he ate by the sounds of the sighted. He felt more tied to humanity.

As he closed the door behind Maria, Renato began to ask about her health again. In hushed tones, conversation was made. After a few minutes, Maria was crying. A few minutes later, she was sobbing uncontrollably.

Finally, Maria ran out of Renato's office and slammed the door behind her, holding her stomach and crying uncontrollably. The beggar beneath the window pounded the ground with his fist and tossed vegetable scraps into the darkness.

For a few moments, Renato held his head in his hands and gazed into the silent darkness that was San Sebastiano by evening. Finally, with a certain, resolute feeling, he rose from his chair, grasped the kneeling stand at which he prayed every morning, and began to work.

For a time, the impenetrable silence and gloom was punctuated by the repeated pounding of hammer on nail. Then, for a time, there was silence.

• • •

It was very late that night. Renato was staring at his creation. Two spikes were sticking through his kneeling stand; a third was sticking through the board upon which he'd normally place his Bible.

Looking at his creation, he decided that all suffering could only occur in silence. First, there was Madrid and now here. He could run no further. Everywhere he moved, he expected to change. Everywhere he moved, he remained the same. He realized now that he was not the victim, he was the predator. He had to be stopped. He knew of no other way to end the pain. He approached his kneeling stand and, with great force and effort, forced his left leg to kneel upon the spike and impaled himself from knee to thigh. The pain was unearthly; his blood ran upon his office floor. He then took his right leg and impaled his right knee up through the thigh. He wanted to scream, but he refused. Finally, he pushed his own neck upon the spike of the board that generally held the Bible. Though blind with pain, he endeavored to pierce his jugular. He did not miss.

• • •

The copper sun which rose over the waters of San Sebastiano that day infused the cirrus clouds with a tangerine tint. Many fishermen were already at the shoreline, preparing their nets for the catch of the day. The banter and jokes of hundreds of years filled the air. The orange boat of Vincenzo was just pushing off from shore when a loud shriek of horror pierced the constancy and changed the tone of the day.

Almost dressed, Jude quickly put his robe overhead and ran toward the scream. He found Maria in the hall outside of Renato's room, crying hysterically with blood on her hands. Jude pushed the door open and saw the horror of his friend's body, and Renato's blood all over the floor. Quickly, he ran across the room and bolted the window shutters. He closed the door and grasped Maria by her shoulders.

"You must compose yourself. This cannot be known by anyone. Go to your room and wash your hands. Wait there for me. Speak to no one."

Without thought, Maria followed the priest's commands; it is what she always did. As her door closed, a few fishermen approached the church, out of breath and with knives in hand.

"What is it, Father Jude? We heard a scream. What has happened?"

Jude waved the men away. "It is nothing. Just Maria. She...she saw a rat so big, it was the size of a cat! She was frightened. It was a big, fat rat, nothing more."

The fishermen laughed with the priest. "A big rat!"

"Yes, yes," they laughed, "a woman scared of a big, fat rat." They returned to the shoreline telling jokes of weak, anxious women they had known.

Jude knew he had to act fast. His friend was dead, but he had no time to mourn him. His best act would be to help his friend die with honor and dignity.

He ran to Renato's room and removed the sheet from his bed. He then brought all of his bedding, along with Renato's bedspread and the white sheet, to the pastor's office.

Horrified by the scene before him, Jude tossed large quilts on the pool of blood to help soak it up from the floor. The door closed behind him, and the shutters bolted as he worked, Jude cried as he lifted his friend's head from the Bible plank and struggled to pull his legs off the spikes in the kneeler. He found a corner of the room where there was no blood and wrapped his friend's body in the white sheet that he had brought for him.

When the floor was clean, he turned to the bloody bedding and the kneeling stand that Renato had constructed. The oven fires were burning high because Maria had recently started them but then discovered Renato's body before she could adjust the flame.

Jude ran to the ovens with the blood-soaked bedding and forced them into the opening that was small and generating heat that Jude found difficult to bear. He then brought the kneeler from Renato's room and used that to push the quilts more deeply into the flames before leaving it in the fire to burn. Finally, he took off his own robe and shoved it into the fire, being careful not to singe his arms while he did.

Locking Renato's office, he ran to his own room to clean up and dress again. Adrenaline was driving each decision he made. He was sad and he was angry, but he had no time for those emotions. He had to calm Maria and orchestrate the death of his great friend.

Finally, clean as he could be and dressed in new vestments, he approached Maria's room. She lay on the bed sobbing uncontrollably. Jude approached her with compassion and caution. He held out his hand to comfort her. Tears were in his eyes as he spoke. "I am so sorry, Maria. So sorry that you had to see him that way." Jude's voice cracked as he spoke, and tears rolled down his cheeks.

Maria could not speak. She continued to sob into her pillow. Jude felt very bad about what he was going to ask her to do. "Maria, I do not know why my friend did this to himself. I know that he was troubled, but I never saw the depth of his despair. Perhaps I helped push him. I mentioned a bad time in life when we were speaking yesterday. Maybe I should not have said anything. I was trying to be supportive." Jude was crying again.

Maria lifted her head from the pillow, and her bloodshot eyes looked at the priest. "I should never have told him."

Through his grief, Jude saw the simple Maria trying to shoulder a burden she did not deserve. He could not let her feel that way. "You mean the lies?"

"You know?" Through her sadness, Maria was astounded.

"Yes, we both heard yesterday."

"My God." Maria's hand moved before her open mouth to mask her shock.

Believing that her sin had been somehow shared with this kind priest by her dear Renato, Maria blushed bright red and returned her head to the pillow, though she cried with less sadness than before.

Jude rubbed her back as he spoke. "You must help me, Maria. You must be strong. We must preserve the memory of my distressed friend."

With a note of resignation, Maria asked what she needed to do. She would do anything for Pietro Renato. Trying to gain control of his composure and the situation, Jude forced himself to plan. "I told the fishermen that you screamed because you saw a large rat. That must be our story. I have cleared the room and burned the bedding. I have burned the…instrument of Renato's destruction." Here Maria burst into tears again. "We need to do a final scrubbing of his floor. I will then make an announcement to the town that he has died suddenly. We will bury him and then move on. Grieve as you would any death of someone dear to you; you must never share with anyone the manner of his death. Can you do that for Pietro Renato, Maria?"

If nothing else, Maria had always been devoted to her priest. She promised that she could help Jude execute his plan. Using a special cleanser that she had concocted out of sea salt and sand, she cleaned Renato's floor. Jude let the townspeople know that Pietro Renato was dead and that he would be buried after a brief Mass that was to be held in the church the very next morning.

After he made his announcement to the fishermen, Jude was accosted by Presario, the man who had provided the fish the night before. "It was not the fish that killed Padre Renato, was it?"

Jude smiled sadly. "It was not the fish, my son."

"Well, Father. There is no place in the cemetery that is right for the good Father Renato. Perhaps we should bury him at sea?"

The thought had never occurred to Jude, and he found it curiously appropriate. The fisherman was right. There was no suitable spot in the cemetery. As far as Jude was concerned, the condition of the cemetery had contributed to his friend's death. He thought that a burial at sea would be perfect.

The next morning, after Mass, the shrouded body of Pietro Renato was brought to sea by the orange boat of Vincenzo Rescrate. After a few brief words of praise, the body was tossed overboard and marked by a floating cross that would be Pietro Renato's tombstone forever. Jude bowed his head in silent prayer. Maria blessed herself repeatedly, kissed the wooden cross around her neck, and held her hands beneath her stomach.

After a time, the fishermen returned their hats to their heads, brought their boats to shore, and looked forward to a new day tomorrow when they could fish again.

Jude was asked by the archdiocese to stay on for a time until a new pastor was found. He started drawing up plans for the renovation of the cemetery. Maria quit her job at the church. The lack of work seemed to wear on her in an odd way. She became lethargic and always seemed to be eating. The men of the town commented that the pretty little girl would grow fat and unattractive—like that big rat—if she didn't stop eating. She did not stop. She wouldn't listen to the townsmen.

Neither Jude nor Maria could anticipate what would happen to the fishermen of San Sebastiano.

The day after Renato was deposited in the sea, the fishermen went out to fish as they always did, confident that a day of holy contemplation upon the sea would yield a great harvest of fish. As the sun set, boat after boat returned to shore without a fish on board. So it was the next day and the day after that and the day after that.

The fishermen became angry and started to weave seemingly unrelated events into harsh coincidences. Presario brings a fish to the priest, the priest dies that night. That dead priest was buried in the waters of San Sebastiano, and the fish disappear. Some said that Presario was an evil man. Presario was shunned by men he had known for years. No one would fish with Presario or near Presario. They asked Jude to absolve the waters of whatever sin or act of heresy it was that drove away the fish. Jude did as they wished, but the fish did not return.

After ten days of barren boats and futile searches for new fishing zones, a group of fishermen went to Jude asking that the body of Renato might be removed from the waters to be buried elsewhere. Jude said that they were being silly and superstitious, but finally he acceded to their requests.

He rode to the floating cross in the boat of Vincenzo. They cast the net overboard and lifted the shrouded body of Renato out of the sea. They rowed back to the shore and reverently placed the pastor's body beneath the tree that Maria loved so well, the tree that Jude made it his business to preserve in the plans for restructuring the cemetery. The heavy lifting and slow work of moving the body had moved daylight into night. Jude blessed the body one more time and told the fishermen that Renato would be interred the next day.

Again, the fishermen removed their caps and blessed themselves, happy that Jude was willing to help them, certain that this was a better place for the priest they loved so well.

All went to bed, tired from the efforts of the day. Sleeping soundly, none could hear the rustling and activity of deep night.

The fishermen greeted the new morning with a newfound enthusiasm for fishing. Nets were filling with fish as soon as they were dropped overboard. Men were struggling to maneuver heavily laden boats to shore. They were convinced that it was the proper treatment of the holy man that caused the fish to return. All were ecstatic.

When Jude rose and went to the cemetery to bury his friend, he was shocked to see nothing but a very damp shroud. He looked for the blind beggar who lived by the gates, but he was nowhere to be found. Footprints surrounded the area where he found the shroud, but Jude felt it best not to follow them. He felt that he had done enough for his friend. He did not feel the need to delve any more deeply into the twisted existence and death of a man that he never really knew. He buried the shroud, erected a small white cross with the name of Pietro Renato on it, and allowed the people of the San Sebastiano to believe that was where the body lay.

Soon his secret wish was granted and he was transferred from the parish of San Sebastiano. Privately, he felt that the place was cursed—too much evil had he seen.

Months later, he passed through the town on his way to visit another friend at a different parish along the shore. He encountered Maria, with a baby in her arms. She said it was hers and that one of the fishermen was the father.

The fishing was as good as it had ever been. All was happy, as it had always been. No one had seen the blind beggar for some time. No one really missed him.

Timothy Harper

Timothy Harper had often felt that the world made more sense without him in it. He had not asked to be born. He felt that he was never welcome in the world, and he was never much amused by the people in it. Why are we forced to live? he wondered. Why must we embrace the capricious whims of the stupid? Timothy never really enjoyed life. He never understood how anyone ever could. He had shared so many empty laughs, felt sympathy for so many temporary and foolish sorrows. Happiness was too superficial to even approach any level of transient importance. The only thing less meaningful than all of this was his work—any time he thought seriously about it, he realized that it meant nothing at all.

Love was never experienced by Timothy Harper. He had had many moments where the illusion of deep caring and shared thought would appear for a time only to dissolve into empty laughs and foolish sorrows.

Alone, next to a tree of many winters, Timothy removed the gun from his waistband, opened his mouth, and blew his brains into the grey bark of the great tree. His body collapsed instantly.

Pheasants in a nearby field scattered at the sound of gunfire. Two deer accelerated their pace and ran toward the clearing where the pheasants had been, then stopped as the slight echo of the loud sound subsided.

The body of Timothy Harper was never found. Eventually his clothing blew away and his bones were carried to remote corners of the forest by various scavenging animals who cared not one bit about the quality of Timothy Harper's existence.

• • •

Francesca Grimaldi loved to apply makeup by candlelight. She lit two slim, white tapers and fit them into the sconces that sat on either side of the round mirror that framed her face. She lightly touched powder to her nose and both cheeks. To give her face life, she gently rubbed on a rouge that had been brought to her from Paris by a man she had loved at a time so long ago. She feathered in amethyst eye shadow and then applied a lavender lipstick that Lord Rodney had given her when she visited him in Tenerife. Growing wistful, she recalled what a lovely time that was.

Upon closer examination, she thought that the ringlet curls that framed her face needed more gel to hold them in position for the evening's festivities, and so she applied it. A closer look at her face revealed a need for more powder, which she subsequently applied.

Her flat chest revealed no cleavage, though the scoop of the lavender gown she was wearing was rather low. She was grateful for the white lace along the neckline. She never wanted her clothing to be too revealing.

Her fingers were long and very thin, as were her arms and her legs. When naked, she looked very much like a skeleton with skin tightly stretched over its bones. Still, men found her attractive. Many wanted to bed her down, and then lavished gifts upon her after the experience. She smiled at the indistinct beauty reflected by the mirror. She looked forward to an evening of great laughs and, perhaps, great love. Francesca blew out the candles by the mirror, reached for her favorite string of pearls, and gently fastened them around her neck. The final step in the process was the hand-painted fan that she'd been given by Alex last summer. It would be the perfect accoutrement for the look she was seeking.

Francesca grasped the ivory knob on the bedroom door and moved to descend the double staircase and join the party which was already in progress.

The staircase led to a large foyer, which had a floor of Italian marble. Upon the walls were classic portraits of great aristocrats long dead.

As Francesca approached, an old man with long white hair and a thick white mustache stood drinking champagne with a buxom woman who wore a gold gown, gold shoes, and a string of eye-catching diamonds around her neck. The centermost diamond lay on the center of her chest and seemed to purposefully direct one's eye to her very ample cleavage.

The man with the long white hair wore a uniform that looked almost naval. The hat was arched in a semicircle with a point at either end, and a large white feather protruded at the back. His double-breasted black shirt had gold buttons that extended from just beneath his shoulders to just above his waist. He also wore gold epaulets that Francesca assumed to be an indication of some rank in the service.

The man was clearly enamored of the large-breasted woman, and Francesca heard him speak in charming tones as she approached.

"Milady, you are the belle of this ball. A gem in a sea of ordinary stones." He reached for the large woman's hand and kissed it gently.

The woman smiled, but did not reply.

Francesca approached them both and introduced herself. The old man did not hide the fact that he evaluated the chest of the woman in gold before he turned to study Francesca.

Still, he managed to smile and kiss Francesca's hand.

The old man approached Francesca and allowed his hand to caress her body as he reached around her waist and planted it upon her side. He whispered to her in her ear as he drew her close.

"I've heard so much about you from the others. You cannot deny me tonight."

Francesca smiled the coquettish smile she had developed over the years. "You've not started well, Sir. I need much more attention, and I will not compete with that cow." Francesca grasped the old man's wrist, removed his hand from her hip, and moved to join the crowd in the ballroom.

The old man looked crushed as he slowly followed her into the room.

The room's air was heavy with the smell of too much expensive perfume, too much aromatic cache. Overweight men danced with lithe, languid women to music that was over 100 years old. Against every wall were tables filled with bottles of alcohol and rich foods.

Francesca grasped a champagne flute as it walked by her held high by the white-coated steward whose brass buttons shined brightly. She sipped from the glass as she surveyed the room. So many men she had loved so many times before. Various men looked at Francesca as they danced by her with other women in their arms.

Finally, she was approached by a swarthy-looking gent with brown curly hair and a brown mustache that curled around the edges of his mouth. His teeth were crooked and yellow from too many cigarettes. He whispered something Spanish into Francesca's ear that made her giggle as he reached around her waist from behind and tried to sneak a peek down the front of her lavender dress.

The man wore a jet black silk shirt with a royal blue sash diagonally placed from his left shoulder to his waist. His pants were very tight, and while lithe, he appeared muscular for his size. There was something very coarse about him. It was not in his manner of dress, which was quite appropriate for the gathering. Rather, there was something eminently earthy in his being that would show through the trappings of any uniform, any manner of dress. Many women found the coarseness exciting and irresistible; Francesca did not. She removed his hand from her pelvis and admonished the young man in Spanish and English. She turned to look at him with cavalier disdain. "There are many more interesting than you, my little friend. Perhaps you should try your immature tricks on one of the others."

Francesca returned her attention to the dancing and a fresh flute of champagne. It was then that she noticed one who seemed different than the rest. He was not in uniform, and he looked very uncomfortable. He wore a yellow button-down dress shirt underneath a camel's hair blazer with blue jeans and brown comfortable shoes that were not at all appropriate for the quality of this event. She wondered if he had received the gold-embossed invitation that was sent to all the others. If he had, why did he not get dressed? If he had not, why did he decide to attend? The curious nature of the strange man interested Francesca. As she moved to approach the man, her upper arm was grasped by a strong, large hand.

"You owe me, my sweet." The voice was instantly recognizable, as was the scent of alcohol on the man's breath. It was the General. He was in full dress uniform, and his silver saber ran beside the olive drab trousers that covered his leg. He pulled the lavender dress to his body and wrapped his arms around Francesca. "Care to dance, my princess?" Pulling her body close to his, he led Francesca around the floor, stumbling only slightly as they danced.

Whenever he was drunk, the General always asked for her. Twirling in circles around the floor, her eye often caught a glimpse of the ill-dressed stranger. Francesca's ability to seem to care about what was before her while actually focusing on something else entirely was a skill that she had spent years developing. It was a skill she had mastered years before. The General was a predictable bore, a repetitive adventure that had the illusion of being quite new when in fact it was trite and quite old. The stranger was the undiscovered country Francesca had spent a life trying to build—could he be the one? She looked for him in the crowd. There was something about him, something odd yet familiar.

The gala had now reached a fever pitch of organized chaos. The long white tapers that had filled the hall with the smoky light of a blue haze from days gone by were reflected in perfectly polished mirrors.

Elegantly dressed women and men in dress uniform twined, untwined, and entwined, dancing to a rhythm of a forgotten day, a long lost elegance. The revelers and music were one, one with each other, one with the music, one with the rhythm of a special night. Francesca had drunk more champagne and danced with more men than any other woman had any right to enjoy. Her eyes glistened in the candlelight. Her jewelry sparkled in the indistinct gloom as the party, the candles, and the revelry began to wind down.

At first a few couples, exhausted from an evening of unrelenting exuberance, began to leave the affair. Arm in arm, or heads rested on shoulders, couples would slowly retire. Not wanting to leave, not caring to stay, they wanted to move to different, more private adventures that couples sometimes share by themselves. Francesca could imagine them folded, one on top of the other, trying one more time to find one more way of experiencing that which substitutes for the ultimate in the tired days and tired ways of what is otherwise known as the ennui of daily existence. Searching for the joy of creation and the bright light of discovery, they found only each other. The existence of the General was so predictable only because it was so common. There is nothing so ugly as a duckling pretending to be a swan.

In the hall, languid women in pastel chiffon dresses lay dazed, exhausted, or drunk across the laps of fine men in their fine suits. It was a poignantly beautiful tableau of the autumn of mankind. The pastel dresses looked like so many dead leaves of fall, strewn as they were over brittle man twigs that were a signpost to a finer day, a younger day, a day less desperately seeking a special day and celebrating night.

The orchestra had already begun to pack their instruments away. Some flirted with the women who were still upright and interested enough to engage. The air smelled of stale champagne, French cigarettes, and perfume-soaked perspiration. The candles were very low now, and Francesca surveyed the scene before her with a smile. She was certain that her foray into elegance and the world of the genteel was an overwhelming success. She was very satisfied with herself and her party. She looked through the wall of windows behind the orchestra and saw the red orange sky of the sunrise. The evening had lasted longer than she had imagined.

It was then that she noticed the man who was dressed in an ordinary way. He was standing between two sconces where the candles were burnt very low. He stood staring at Francesca. In the shade of the sconces his eyes appeared to be small bright lights focused on the woman before him. The intensity of his stare and the inappropriate garb had reawakened her curiosity, and she shambled toward the dark stranger with a smile.

"Who are you? Why are you not dressed? What brings you to this gala tonight? I don't think that I invited you, but I am very glad that you came." She had been slowly approaching the stranger as she spoke. He stood rooted to the floor, not saying a thing.

Her eyes glistening, she moved to unbutton the top button of the stranger's shirt, and he pulled away slightly. She smiled and then pursed her lips slightly, admonishing the young man before her. "Please don't pull away from me; a young virile man like yourself is quite interesting to me." She opened the second button of his shirt and stepped more closely to the man before her.

For a moment the candles on either side of his head flared slightly, perhaps awakened by the passion that Francesca was feeling, the intensity she was trying to awaken in the young man before her.

The young man stared into the face of the woman before him. Did she really not know? He saw every crevice that was filled with the powder, the black circles beneath her eyes that were grey from all the makeup she had placed atop them. The thin wrinkled neck, the liver spots that she tried so hard to cover up. Her hands were wrinkled and showed veins and arteries crossing over bones that flared at her knuckles. Did she not know? Could she really not see? He moved his face closer to hers to give her another chance. Francesca made the mistake that many make who are used to living life in just one way. She reacted in the way to which she was accustomed.

She wrapped her arms around the man before her, kissed him on the cheek, and then tried to engage his lips. "Come with me," she said. "We'll go up to my room."

Though his mind was a cacophony of pain and outrage, the young man went with Francesca. It was he, after all, who had initiated this thing, wanting to know all that he could about her. He, who had stolen the invitation to find the place. The place he had heard so much about. The place he could not believe existed. He wanted to see the "real Francesca" one more time. It was he who believed this would somehow help.

He ascended the steps with Francesca as she entwined her arm in his and rubbed her breast against him. He allowed her to kiss his neck and his cheek, and he didn't know why. It was a big decision he was about to make, and he had to be sure.

Slowly, sensually, Francesca opened the door to her bedroom and invited the young man in. She lit a gaslight lamp on a bedside table and pulled back the crimson drapes which surrounded her bed. She reached out to pull the young man down on top of her, but he resisted. His mind was throbbing. The pain and the outrage were unbearable.

Francesca smiled softly, "I've seen young men like you before, soft, tentative, embarrassed. She placed her hands out and massaged his thighs. I can help you overcome this and give you great joy."

The young man was flushed, feeling overwhelmed. "Then you've been doing this for a long time?" The timbre of his voice was choppy. He seemed to be losing control.

"I have been here for over thirty years, do I look it?" She smiled coquettishly as she began to remove her rings and bangles of jewelry—leaving only the choker around her neck.

The young man felt that if he moved at all, he might explode. As she removed each piece of jewelry, the young man saw another wrinkle, another matrix of lines on her old and matronly skin. Why was he here? Why did he decide he had to do this? He felt like he was about to cry.

Francesca removed her dress and hung it on the headboard of her bed. She lay naked before him except for the necklace that still glistened in the candlelight. The young man moved to approach her as the door to the bedroom flew open and an old man approached the bed with his shirt and pants open—it was the General.

"Where is she? You are mine tonight, my dear. We romp at dawn." Francesca laughed at the obviously drunk and overly exuberant man, and screamed slightly as he jumped upon her bed.

"Excuse me, my dear General, but there seems to be someone in line before you." Francesca pointed to the young man whose eyes were wide with horror.

"Did he pay? Did you pay as handsomely as I did, dear boy? Well? Speak up, young man!"

The young man shook his head "no"; he did not know what else to do. This had all taken such a horrible turn that he could bear no more.

"Well, then." The General removed his clothing and tossed it in a pile in the center of the room. "You're welcome to watch if you'd like, but she is mine." The General proceeded to mount Francesca in a manner so inelegant that it only could be considered brutishly drunk.

As the General began the proceedings, Francesca looked over his shoulder at the young man before her. She could see tears running down his cheeks. Was it a moment of inadvertent excitement generated by the activity of the general, or was it a different realization that made Francesca shout suddenly as a look of shock overtook her face?

The young man looked one more time at the lady before him and ran out of the bedroom door, down the stairs, and out of the house. He would never return again.

Sixteen years ago, he'd spent countless hours defending her house, fighting for her dignity. Sixteen years ago, she'd said it would be best for him. He'd get out and they'd be together again. She just had to free him from the inappropriate behavior of the father he'd never met. For sixteen years, he'd been fighting, defending the indefensible. Now he knew the truth.

He had been thrust out of her world because he was inconvenient. He knew that now. She had written and told him that she cared, but she never really cared. She had lied to him just as she had lied to herself. She lived, she lied. He always felt that the world made more sense without him in it. He finally had the courage to do something about it. At least she gave him that.

www.ingramcontent.com/pod-product-compliance
Lightning Source LLC
Chambersburg PA
CBHW070309260626
47160CB00003B/781